6S

SIX SENTENCES

Volume 1

CONTENTS

for Jill

Pre-Flight Announcement

by Robert McEvily

Hello and welcome aboard Flight 6 – this is your pilot speaking. Please stow your personal prejudices in the overhead compartments, and be sure to unpack your open-mindedness. If this is your first time flying with us, a note of warning: you can never know for sure what to expect on this flight. Just look around – you'll notice all kinds of people from all over the world, with an array of opinions, perspectives, and writing styles. During our flight together, the weather may be sunny or cloudy, or stormy, or all three at once – *boom*, just like that. So fasten your seatbelts, settle in, and be prepared – it's gonna be a *wild* flight...

Part 1

Takeoff

The Star-Lite Bowlerama

by Brian Steel

Millie Metuchen is the sole employee of the Star-Lite Bowlerama in Lebanon, Missouri, and on this Tuesday night in June, standing behind the orange Formica countertop of the food stand, she is fighting the urge to cry. The bowling alley is almost empty, just four teenagers double-dating and laughing and munching on the mini-frozen pizzas she had almost burnt a moment before in the old toaster oven beside her. The popcorn machine stands idle and the parking lot is empty below the flashing neon sign that spells out *Bowl-er-am-a!* But it is the young man in the checkered cowboy shirt playing pool that Millie has been watching. He's an out-of-towner from the motel across the road and as he walks around the table and lines up a shot, he looks just like a boy she once knew in high school who left Lebanon and moved to Springfield to sell cars at the Ford dealership and hasn't been back since, not even to visit. Under the counter, between the straws and Styrofoam cups, there's an old bottle of gin she keeps stashed away, for emergencies such as this.

Tiny Girl Violence

by Shaindel Beers

Sometimes she likes to lie in bed and remember every cruel thing that's ever been said to her — the boyfriend who snarled, "Sex with you would be easier if each of your thighs didn't weigh in at nine thousand pounds;" the one who had yelled over the phone, "If I'm going to work on not being selfish, I'm going to do it for me, not for you." She wished she could become a superhero, of sorts. She'd carry a purse-sized branding iron with her that would read TGV in small Garamond type and brand her victim each time she overheard a man humiliate a woman. In time, men would grow to fear Tiny Girl Violence, and the men would be marked, the way they deserved. If a woman was taking off his shirt for the first time, and she saw the letters under a dancing cross or St. Brendan medal or Star of David dangling from a chain, she'd know. And she would make her escape, swiftly, quickly; and he would never know what hit him.

A Mother's Love

by Heather Leet

I carry the baggage of her life around with me everywhere I go. It is a heavy burden and although I have often dreamed of setting it down and walking away, I do not, I persevere. She loved me I know but that love is the heaviest piece of luggage that I carry. It drags me down so far that I no longer go in large bodies of water for fear it will drag me down to the bottom and I will drown with her love. I often wonder what will happen with all of her bags when I die. I look at the beautiful face of my daughter and I pray that she has the strength that I do not and throws these bags on the trash heap of the past where they belong.

In My Darkened Bedroom

by Chi Sherman

After a long, hot shower, I rub almond oil into my skin, circling the oval indentation that is my navel, running my hands up and around my breasts, down my belly, sweeping feather-soft strokes across my thighs. My right hand traces my collarbone and I imagine a tattoo of stars in hues of blue tripping their way across the bone. I bend to administer to my calves, my feet, running my fingers across my toes until they shine in the bathroom light, massaging the corded muscles that run through my thighs as I ease out tension from dancing for hours the night before. I admire my sideways stance when I glance in the mirror, my ass round and full, warm beneath my hands as I smooth the dips and hollows of my curves. Leftover oil pools in my palms and I rub it through my thick, dark tresses, smiling at myself in the mirror as I wrap myself in a thick, lavender towel. In my darkened bedroom, I run my hands over my body as I stretch my right leg towards the ceiling, flex my foot, point my toes, and think of the lover who will someday come into my life, a woman who will ease her way up my body from toes to crown, sink her teeth into me with a grin, who will embrace this serenity.

Untitled #1

by Michael Lipkowitz

Sometimes you'll wake up with memories of your dreams. You lie in bed for what seems like hours at a time, immersed in these fleeting sensations that never leave. They are like traces, footprints of something greater: the warmth of your breath on the skin of her neck (her skin felt like lilacs in the cool night); the way the wind blows around you as walk with her on an uneventful Thursday, your shoes soggy from the warm rain; the way she smiles when you call her beautiful, the way you can hear her smile, even over the phone. Because her happiness has a sound, a distinct sound, a subtle but powerful sound that could deafen even the Sirens. And the moments spent with her were eternal. You had those moments trapped in between your cupped hands like a firefly; you could hear the silent fluttering of wings, feel the gentle movement of wiry antennae against your soft skin, but to look, to glimpse the beauty, was to lose it forever to the night.

Homeland Insecurity

by Joseph Grant

In an effort to combat the war on terror, the Government has issued the following statement: "An unidentified flying object maneuvering at will in and out of restricted air space, its transponder apparently turned off and not replying to repeated FAA requests for the aircraft to identify itself, was shot down by the US military over the Midwest. Local and federal authorities were quick to locate a bewildered and oddly dressed old man who appeared unhurt and apparently spoke no English. He was surrounded by a pack of nine wild reindeer, one with an obviously burned snout acquired from the fiery crash site. In an apparently unrelated event, hundreds of thousands of toys were discovered scattered from here to Kalamazoo. The bearded man was being detained and checked out by Homeland Security and INTERPOL as he was found on his person a list of many names, some classified and put on a 'bad' list, as well as many maps with 'x' marks scrawled upon them and carrying what one unidentified policeman said were many 'foreign-sounding aliases,' which were given to the local press as Father Christmas, Sinter Klaas, Babbo Natale, Black Peter, Jultomten, Grandfather Frost, Kris Kringle, Shengdan Laoren, Pere Noel, as well as many other un-American sounding assumed names. It is not clear as this story went to press whether or not the man spreading dangerous ideologies such as 'Peace on Earth' and 'Good Will Towards Man' and "To All a Good Night" would be held at the terrorist detainment center at Guantanamo Bay."

If I Were to Kill Myself

by Bryce Carlson

If I were to kill myself, I would want to do so in the most elaborate fashion because if I'm going out, I'm going out with some serious style. I'm talking: fireworks, nudity, flying through the air, dancing, loud flatulence, a potato gun loaded with one potato, some Skittles, a disposable camera with two pictures left, a mouthful of cashews, and a hundred dollar bill cut perfectly in half. I would definitely have to do something wild, something like light off a bunch of fountain fireworks at the top of an insanely tall building before jumping off completely naked with: a loaded potato gun and a disposable camera both around my neck, a handful of cashews in my mouth, a bag of Skittles candy in one hand, and a perfectly cut in half hundred dollar bill in the other. As I flew through the air, I would dance and pass gas so that I could smile when I take the last two pictures in the disposable camera before opening the package of Skittles so that the candies can fall with me. The finale would be me shooting the potato gun straight into the air above me before the following happens: I smash onto the concrete with my back while Skittles shower around me, people see the cashews in my mouth and say "He's nuts," someone takes the disposable camera to get it developed and see the last moments of my life, two other people find the halves of the hundred dollar bill and try to use them only to find out that you need more than half of a bill for it to be accepted, and a potato suddenly coming out of nowhere to explode somewhere close to me between twenty seconds and a minute after I shower the concrete with my naked body. I would do something like that if I were to kill myself.

Try to Remember

by Diane Brady

"Good evening, Mrs. Smith, my name is Margaret, and I want to congratulate you on winning our Great Show Tune Getaway For Two in New York City; the judges selected a classic for you, Mrs. Smith, and to claim the prize you must sing the chorus to a Broadway song ~ *Try to Remember* ~ from *The Fantasticks*. No, that's the name of the song, Mrs. Smith - *Try to Remember*; oh, you lost your voice screaming during the Super Bowl last night; I don't care how your voice sounds; I just want to hear the lyrics; do you *follow* me? Yes, Mrs. Smith, you did enter the contest; I have your entry right in front of me; no, I'm not sure what box you placed it in; we collect entries from boxes at state fairs, shopping malls and gas stations all over the country; just sing that chorus, please. Yes, it's an old song; no, I'm not sure of the year; I wasn't even born when the show opened; I don't know the melody; all I can see on my screen is the chorus that you, Mrs. Smith, must sing to claim the prize. No, you cannot call your neighbor for help; I understand your predicament; no, this is not a prank call, Mrs. Smith; yes, I really have your entry on my desk; it has a mustard stain on it; you were probably eating a hot dog at a state fair; oh, you never eat mustard; you haven't been out of the house much all year. That could be an explanation, Mrs. Smith; his secretary always travels with him on business and entered the contest using your name; yes, I understand; my husband was a lyin', cheatin' bum who disappeared a year ago and left me with three kids to support; yeah, I took this ridiculous telemarketer job at night to pay the rent; I have an idea, Mrs. Smith; we could do the trip together; I really need a vacation; you can't think of the words; well, I've been staring at them on my screen for the past twenty minutes and practically have them memorized; the chorus is really simple, Mrs. Smith; do you *follow* me?"

The Show Me State

by Quin Browne

His service was held on a Monday, the same day as his birth, as it was the only day the colour guard was able to fly into the small Missouri town where they lived, where he'd be laid to rest; she gave in gracefully, in spite of her feeling the same day of the week coincidence was a sacrilege in her eyes. She held up through the ceremony, only shuddering the once when the guns went off, smiling the soft smile he loved so when they gave her the flag and thanked her for the life he'd given in a war he didn't care about one way or the other; she believed in honouring the warrior. She put her arm around her husband, holding him close, when he sobbed as the dirt hit the casket, knowing he would never recover, never have that look of pride again when he spoke of their children - there was a hole in the fabric of their future. She washed and dried and returned casserole dishes and pie plates and Tupperware, thanking the owner with a small note for the time and love that went into the gift of food one always sends with the announcement of death. She finally stopped holding up, stopping holding in, allowing herself to sink to the ground and keen her pain, her loss, her anger that day in March, when the sound of his laughter in her heart stilled. There, on the front porch, she lay in the bitter wind that carried her cries as it ruffled the pages of the letter requesting compensation for his faulty body armour that hadn't saved him, calling it *equipment left behind on the battlefield* - in this war, a pound of flesh wasn't payment enough.

The Distraction

by E.Y. Kwee

Her interviewer looked like Elijah Wood. This was important; it was a college interview and it would have a significant effect on her future as her mother had kept reminding her — rather annoyingly — in the car. But his shirt was light blue and his eyes crinkled at the edges when he smiled; when he smiled, she saw Sam, and Aragorn, and Orlando Bloom with his enhanced elfin ears, and Liv Tyler as the elfin princess and she saw the world that she had ached to belong to after watching all three *Lord of the Rings* movies in a blurry row. He tapped his pen when he was thinking and subtly scrawled inky blue notes like slanted, uber-thin ribbons across his interview sheet when he thought she wasn't looking. She felt vaguely uncomfortable at his expressionless eyes — sucked dead by these interviews, most likely — and swiveled in her chair, tapped her feet against the bar on the table, hating how her feet couldn't touch the floor on these pretentious, coffee-shop stools. There awkwardness floating in the empty air — the awkward turtle was making an ungainly appearance — and as he made a comment about the false Santa sitting on the chair a few feet away from them, under the heat and commotion of the gaudy gilded olive Christmas tree and its tinsel decorations and shimmery lights and the lines of lights like unnaturally bright crystal raindrops hanging from the ceiling, she tried to draw her mind back in the conversation to answer the next question — tell me about your high school — but it was no use, because he smiled, and she thought again, *my interviewer looks like Elijah Wood.*

Twelve Roses

by Jamie Boyt

My love. I wanted to do something special for you, to show you how much you mean to me, how much I love you. A dozen red roses, in yellow, the colour of love, just like you told me, remember? One for each of the eleven glorious years we have spent together. And one more, just for the hell of it. Now, any chance of a blow job?

Get to Know Me

by Margery Daw

I never exaggerate. I'm non-competitive, which I think gives me an advantage over most people. I'm not into status or one-upmanship; I'm above that, and frankly I look down on people who aren't. I believe in peacefulness, and maintaining a flexible attitude, and I am 100% committed to fighting for those beliefs. I take pride in my humility. But I'm sure this really reveals so little - everybody knows actions speak louder than words.

Hanging with a New Crowd

by Steve Talbert

Sorry, Rod, Elton, Billy and Bob! You were all good to me during my formative years and early adulthood, but one can only listen to "Maggie May," "Rocket Man," "It's Still Rock and Roll to Me" and "Old Time Rock and Roll" so many times. Don't worry, though, I haven't disowned you: Although we don't hang out like we used to in the old days, I'll still visit you occasionally. If you are wondering what happened to me, I've been spending my time with a different bunch, including Garth, Randy, Reba and Willie. If you had asked me five years ago, I would've said that country sucks. Now, I know that country music doesn't suck; there's more to it than drinking beer and getting divorced.

A Stranger

by Melody Gray

We left the nightclub, and walked to the restaurant next door for a slice of pizza, laughing, with the music from the band still playing in our ears. She was walking towards me, her friend's arm wrapped around her, and her eyes fixed on mine ready to tell me a secret, like she was waiting all night to let it out. Her arms reached out to me, "My baby is dead, a year ago today, and he is gone." Her friend tried to take her away not knowing how I would react; her skin was a different color than mine and in my town that counts for something no matter what your pain is. "She's okay," the friend attempted to reassure me, but she needed something; she needed to tell someone, anyone who would listen. "I'm sorry for your pain, for your loss," and I take her in my arms for just a moment in time as we passed each other on that street, and she walked away having shared with me, a total stranger, a piece of her pain.

Stray Thoughts

by Peggy McFarland

Last month, she held her infant close, gently sniffed the newborn smell, stroked the soft skin and marveled at the slight pulse in the soft spot on the skull. For a moment, she imagined poking her finger in that tender area just to feel the slight resistance before the gratifying burst as the skin tore; wondering if the gray matter would be warm and spongy on her thumb ~ horrified, she backed away from that vision and kissed the downy scalp instead. Last week, while serving the balding suit his third martini, she felt his chubby, sweaty hand grasp hers. For a moment, she imagined grabbing the empty vodka bottle by the neck, smashing it against the bar and slashing the jagged edges across his sagging jowls, feeling the soft flesh give before it accented his leer with cheeky, bleeding smiles ~ intrigued, she yanked her hand from his grasp, mouthed 'thank you' and winked as she gave him his change. Last night, her boyfriend came home, sniffed the air and complained about dinner. For a moment, she imagined yanking the cast-iron pot off the stove and slamming the flat bottom against his gaping hole, crunching delicate facial cartilage and cracking his two-thousand-dollar crowns; the gentle, bubbly sound of simmering replaced by harsh, gurgling breaths before his body thudded to the saucy, bloody tiles ~ satisfied, she tested the guilt, delighted it didn't dilute the sheer joy of giving in to impulse.

He Died as He Lived

by Eric Spitznagel

My dad died of a massive heart attack - brought on,
the doctors told us, by an enlarged heart. The cause
of death inspired some people, usually well-meaning
friends and family, to put a positive spin on our
tragedy. "He died as he lived," they'd tell us, "with a
big heart." They were just trying to make us feel
better, I suppose, but we didn't want to be cheered
up. So my brother and I stopped telling people about
the enlarged heart and began announcing that he
had, in fact, died from bowel cancer. Try to make a
sentimental aphorism out of *that*.

Biodegradable Woman

by Bob Jacobs

My wife is biodegradable. She's been biodegrading ever since the day she slipped off her wedding dress. She's got a mouth full of fillings, bushy eyebrows, buttocks the size of Belgium, and breasts that hang like secondhand balloons half-filled with custard. Don't get taken in by that 'for better or for worse' crap, because there's not a woman alive who looks better at fifty than she did at twenty-five (or you'd have married her mother) and no amount of flesh hanging down from her upper arms will help. There was a time when she held cigarettes seductively between slender fingers, crimson lips blowing smooth plumes of smoke in a way that whispered *I am what your dreams are made of*, but now she shuffles from room to room in a cumulus haze, slippers dragging across the carpet. Last night, Jesus Christ, she complained that I can't get it up any more.

A Lick of Justice

by Rachel Green

Justice? Was it justice that a man walks free after killing my child? Is a suspended sentence for driving with eleven times the legal limit of alcohol justice for the death of a teenager? Timmy, my lad, had already got a place at the London Conservatory for his skill with the violin – gifted, they said he was – and now he's buried in the churchyard under a yew. I wanted him to feel how I feel, your Honour. That's why I firebombed his house with his whole family asleep inside it.

High Flyer

by Linda Simoni-Wastila

My very atoms vibrate: from caffeine, from sleep deprivation, from the constant moving forward. From erratic consumption of my mood regulators. But my mind is sharp, focused; my dreams, Technicolor wonders. Everything I touch explodes from this magical, sub-cellular energy surging within me. When I press on the closed hollow-wood door to my shrink's office, it flies open with a bang, the knob gouging the plaster wall. He sits at his desk, the room dim but for the green glow of a single lamp, head down, not noticing my tumult.

Retribution

by Jon Cable

Madga's black dragon sat heavily upon its haunches, its giant chin resting contentedly upon the open window sill of her room in the castle tower, drooling gobs of acid onto the stone-worked floor, sizzling like oil in a smoking hot pan. The village of Toulan was a mass of raging fires, houses and shops burning beyond control, smoke and embers all but blotting out the moon hanging low on the horizon. Magda was unaware of the carnage behind her, staring out over the lake stretched out, star flecked and smooth, beneath her. "Today was a long day, Exitus, but I had a nice rest and I feel much better." One hand under her chin, the other idly scratching the coarse hair jutting between the scales of the young dragon's head, she stared up at the stars captured blurrily upon the calm surface of the lake. "I suppose I shall go back tomorrow morning and apologize to that charming old silk vendor for losing my temper, and that wretched look you gave him for raising his voice at me."

Ginsberg's Harmonium

by Peter Wild

Harry was clean, had been clean very nearly 40 days when he spied the harmonium through the grubby storefront window on 26 Second Avenue. It stopped him in his tracks, which was surprising; it wasn't like he was a musician or anything. There was a guy loitering in the doorway, a kid, one of those kids, the hippy lot, with hair round his shoulders and that, you know, vacant cast to his eyes, like as if he'd just emerged from a dope fug for a breath of fresh air prior to diving down to the deepest depths once more, who (spotting that Harry's eye had been caught by the harmonium) jerked his chin up by way of hello and said, "'S'a beautiful thing, aint it?" "Mm," replied Harry, itching his lower right arm with his fidgety left hand, somewhat discombobulated, gripped as he was by a sudden and violent urge to push the kid to one side, grab the harmonium and run, run, run like the rabbit, as if his life depended on it. The kid was talking *rapidemente* about how some fella name of Ginsberg had donated the harmonium for them to use in their *church* - and Harry, itchy Harry, his tongue already too big for his mouth, stood and gawped, befuddled by what the kid was saying (*a church ? this place was a church ? getouttahere*) but wanting the harmonium like he'd never wanted anything before and not even truly understanding why, just knowing that it was something he had to have, had to had to *had to*. Of course he stole it, of course, because stealing was what Harry did best, stealing was what Harry had done best for the majority of his adult life, when he wasn't doing time - and sometimes even when he was doing time - but unlike everything else Harry had ever stolen, the harmonium didn't make him happy, quite the opposite in fact, the harmonium made Harry miserable, drove him crazy, he couldn't sleep with such a beautiful object so close by showing up everything else in his life for the dull, drab, shapeless shit it was and so he sold that harmonium for something like thirty-four bucks and he blew the dough on blow, falling off the wagon and falling so hard he couldn't ever right himself again.

514

by Deborah O'Neal

Empty house, you were so glad, however tentatively, to have the scent and warmth of people moving in, hanging on your long-bare walls the ornament of first one celebration, then another, and another. Your water ran, your windows gleamed, your floorboards creaked with weight and activity; doors were opened, lights were lit, and cool then warm air coursed through your open rooms. People laughed and glasses clinked; you heard again the squeak of the old glider bench; some nights, you watched a fire blaze from the pit in your backyard. A flag was hung, another; you had your picture taken time and again; dressed again with care, with returning awareness of your beauty. Always, there was music, of the people you had now, even when the visits grew scarce and sometimes sad. The music played when the doors stopped opening, the aching of the silence almost more than you could bear, but it played on and it plays now, when you are empty once again.

The Accident

by Robert Prinsloo

The car hit the tree head-on. The airbags deployed, though the passenger landed up under hers and the driver's had only deflected him from his steering wheel. He was thrown through the windshield, without his pants, glass confetti in his hair, his neck broken. And the passenger was crumpled up under the dashboard, her head lolling across the divide and over the driver's pedals, strangled. She wore a pair of suit pants around her neck like a scarf. Like sneezing, the driver should have held back till after the bend in the road.

Twelve Noon Siren

by Monica McFawn

Every morning in the summer when I was a nine or ten, I would walk uptown to the Party Store to put twenty-five cents into the twenty-five cent trinket machine after which the twelve noon siren would sound. The fire station was right across the street, so the initial high peals of the siren were very loud, but then the sound would begin to get lower and quieter. The end of the siren was painfully protracted and profoundly strange. It went on and on and on and sounded to me like a sinister, endless mumble that crept closer the quieter it got. Even when it ended, if it ever did, it felt like that sound was at the back of everything, a rattled-off lower than bass assertion that things were not right. I thought I would never stop hearing the end of the siren but then I became distracted by a horse on my walk home, and forgot until the following noon.

Welcome to Dinner

by L.R. Cooper

"What are you doing," I asked the man standing to my left. He looked at me with a wide-open stare and a dark look on his face. *Those eyes*, I thought to myself, *I've seen them before. Where am I? What is going on? Why is everyone looking at me like I'm Thanksgiving dinner?*

Nothing Ventured, Nothing Gained

by Elizabeth Murray

It was amazing what they both understood yet would never say as their hands accidentally touched in front of their respective partners; intriguing how the simple passing of a pen could ignite and smolder something so sweet. They both boxed the moment inside a Perspex memory, and peered in daily; their secret anchor to their sense of self. Magnified by the silence, each swam freely swathed in the knowledge that someone longed for their touch again. Beyond the monotony of discussions about bills, work and food, they were wanted. They were desired. Both celebrated golden anniversaries, but their hands never touched again.

With an East Texas Drawl

by Doug Wacker

"Sometimes, that grey dust that collects on the side of the road, it kicks up with the wind. It infests every pore of your skin, the inside of your nose, the roof of your mouth. It even gets in the back of your eyeballs and I'll tell you, I can't stand it. I don't know why the hell I ever came to this town in the first place. I figure it had something to do with a woman." Ed spat on the sidewalk and staggered down the road towards the Rusty Dart, where he planned to drink a few whiskeys and forget about things.

Paper Cuts

by Tara Lazar

Her daughter was achingly beautiful, a delicate loveliness like a paper lantern, illuminated from within. Her long hair separated into fine ringlets, like curled Christmas ribbon cascading down her back. She was the kind of child that made strangers smile and take pause – the kind of child that made other mothers envious. The mother was not so much shunned as politely excluded; excuses were made, apologies provided, but invitations were never extended. She exaggerated her own ordinary features – forgoing makeup, leaving her hair unwashed for days, wearing mismatched clothing – but none of her efforts to elicit pity served to lesson the jealousy; her daughter's radiance only shone brighter, her extraordinary hair the source of more disdain. The mother closed her eyes, held the scissors, and cut.

Lost

by Rob Winters

The ledge on the roof is a useless element of this building. It serves one purpose: the ledge is there because it adds some grandeur to the building. An ironic idea by a company on which the irony is lost completely. I've lived an unfulfilling life with the scar of rejected love and intoxicated by the lie that is this society, at times strangely appealing, but not now. Now I have a last desire, to leave and see the parasite that has lured me into a false sense of happiness defeated. Then I will see the real world one last time: grey smoke, corruption so thick you can touch it and all the sins of men on a silver platter, then I jump.

Two Materialists on a Boat

by Tim Horvath

It starts as a joke at a gallery opening, one of those catered affairs where the food is art and the art virtual confectionery, and they form scrums of erudition and talk about the nude parties at Yale and eventually someone says, "You want a scenario that's never been, I'll give you a scenario that's never been: two materialists on a boat, discussing the Yankees after a Jasper Johns show." A bet is placed, odds laid accordingly. Some patron says, "I'm a materialist for starters, anyone care to sneak on board the U.S.S. Intrepid tonight?" Note that there isn't a single Jasper Johns painting on the premises, which proves only the first obstacle; they are agnostics and Buddhist spiritualists and a Catholic clinging to her faith like a hangnail, and there's the gang. The crowd splinters, and the materialist winds up walking up wind-whipped Tenth with one of the agnostics, talking about the ignominious fate of the Mets and about Gerald Miles, one of the featured artists, whose fake catalogues of invented painters stole the show: rows of postcard-sized paintings indistinguishable from shrunken canvases, complete with periods, false starts and aberrations. The materialist stops short and practically yells that while this is hardly the state of affairs he put his money on, the existence of the

Jasper-Johns-boat-thing is strongly implied by the one-to-one correspondence of this reality to the elements in the now-infamous utterance, even if each requires a substitution, but his companion has already stopped, himself, ten steps earlier, and though he is only (as he will go on to explain) memorizing the number of a self-storage place on the side of a building, he sure as hell looks like he is praying.

Eddie Comes and Goes

by Nathan Tyree

Father never speaks, he just sits perched in the lazy boy, looking ahead at nothing. I come and go; I attend school, take care of the house, make my meals, and wait. Father sat in that chair on the day mother left, shouting her mad eyes out the door with a slam. He hasn't moved at all since then. I miss the way he used to laugh, and hug me. He's starting to stink.

Ted and Sylvia Sitting in a Tree

by Sara Crowley

He ripped her hair band off and she bit his cheek. They married and wrote poetry, made babies. She was sad and creative, he was magnetic and creative. He had an affair and she kicked him out. She wrote a lot of good bitter poems, and then she killed herself because it was cold and she was depressed. They loved each other.

Affirmation

by Teresa Tumminello Brader

I'm getting married again, I tell my husband, and he looks at me as if he understands. I'll wear the ivory-colored dress that still hangs in the closet, I think. The church will be full, and the man who wasn't free to marry me years ago will be sitting in a pew with his wife and grown daughter. I visualize the dress being two sizes too small now, so I don't bother fetching it from its hanger. My low-cut, floor-length brown with its empire folds will have to do. "I'm staying," I tell my husband, and he takes me in his arms.

The Dirk

by Adam J. Whitlatch

"What is it you are making there?" asked the blacksmith as he approached the forge where his young apprentice pounded away at his work. "It is a dirk, master," said the young apprentice, holding up the glowing chunk of iron. "It was going to be a surprise for you, but now I guess the secret is out." The blacksmith beamed with pride at his student, "You are a good boy, but be sure to put all of your heart into it, because crafting weapons requires much dedication." *Oh, indeed I shall,* thought the apprentice. *All the sweeter when I put it into your heart, old man.*

The Silent Dream Stealer

by Darrick H. Scruggs

Procrastination is a big word for a reason, it needs to be understood and the magnitude of the damage that can come from being a procrastinator. If you look at all the *would-of's* and *could-of's* in our life, where would we all be if they were *I-did's*? It is amazing: when I reflect on the most difficult times in my life, they usually came from something I put off, or something I waited until the last minute to do, and now I expect the world to align with me due to my procrastination. I consider myself a man of action - most marvel at what I can accomplish in a 24 hour period of time - but my worst trait is procrastination. I once asked an associate why he felt I am not a millionaire... my knowledge base and skill sets are second to none, my people skills are extraordinary, so *why*... he went back to that word procrastination again. If procrastination is keeping you from obtaining the success you deserve, put a plan together today to kill the silent dream stealer, *today*, not tomorrow, because if you wait until tomorrow, the curse of the silent dream stealer will still be alive and well.

Half Hearted Healing

by Amanda Lattin

I just want to hear his heartbeat today, not recall it
from memory, not dream it, but feel it right next to
my own. "Please," I ask, "just lie down with me
today." He considers my request, asks what's going
on, why I'm so sad, and a tight pain rises in my chest;
I was hoping he would understand; I was hoping he
needed to feel my heart for the same sad reasons, so
we could crawl inside one another and at least not be
alone in the determined confusion we call our lives.
The tears are coming back as I reply, "Because of
things I can not change, because when I am old and
you are dead, I want to look back on this day and be
able to remember what your heart sounded like, not
what work we did... is that reason enough?" His tired
eyes meet mine and I know it is reason enough, but
he stands instead; he feels the way to heal a heart is to
deny it, to rise above its weaknesses and hold on to
responsibility in order to make one's self strong – so I
must be his heart in the times he loses his. Finally,
when his gifted hands have accomplished enough and
I ask again with all of the pull of my love, he lies
down and I am allowed to hear the soft strong beat I
will seek out in the wind when we are both gone;
then, as our breath and blood find the same rhythm,
the walls between us melt as does my clinging

sadness; I kiss him, and with the taste of his beautiful presence on my lips, I whisper, "Thank you."

She Loves a Project

by Rebecca Pigeon

She never thought of herself as being overly particular; the front she presented to the world was altogether laid back, unless things didn't go her way. People naturally made comparisons between her and her four other siblings and the results always came out in her favor. She never thought to examine her own character, but as it turns out, she had been a pushy, exacting, know-it-all the whole time. When she drove the last of her friends away with her superior tone and infuriating compassion, she sat down on her perfectly chosen couch and admired her territorial view with a sense of relief. She decided that arranging furniture was far more fulfilling than arranging people's lives. And besides that, chairs and coffee tables stayed where you put them.

Missing You

by Harry B. Sanderford

Luke reached down and switched on the pickup's radio... *erectile dysfunction effects one in...* cringed and gave the knob a twist... MY MONEY, MY BITCHES, MY... then one more half-spin... *take another little piece of my heart now, Ba-Bee!* Janice had work for him; he gave a sideways glance; detecting no objection, he thumbed the volume up a touch. Returning his attention to the road, Luke was dumbfounded to see illuminated in his headlights what appeared to be an Indian brave in buckskin and war-paint clutching the reins of his rearing pinto in one fist and thrusting his befeathered lance into the night with the other. The truck bore down fast; in the time it took Luke to move his foot from the accelerator to the brake they were nearly upon the wayward warrior. Lightning flashed and Luke braked hard, yanking the wheel right and avoiding a collision so narrowly he made eye contact with the now electric brave. Even as he fought for control of the careening vehicle, Luke's mind etched a surreal image of the warrior on horseback, his lips peeled back in the gaping grimace of his war-cry... *"Whaa-Hah uh TAKE IT!"*

Home

by Li-Ann Wong

Where is Home? Home can be a piercingly beautiful Sydney sky atop the Bridge; ships sailing in, white lines trailing, into your Harbour. Home can be the dim yellow lights highlighting the haphazard pathways, disaster of city planning, yet, the bilingual signs, sometimes tri - malay, english, chinese - signal, almost insistently, that you, the prodigal child, have returned. The places could be worlds away, but the feeling is constant - here you are, anchored, tranquil, docked, at peace. A friend said to me, yes, Sydney may be clean and ordered, though seeming to lack a certain character, while Kuala Lumpur, with its filth and arguable seediness, may conceal a certain glorious something that compels one to discover. For the Global Nomad such as I though, Home does not always have to be tangible, for Home... is where the heart is.

It's Just Sex, Baby

by Sarah Flick

James the brilliant architect had dimples when he smiled that matched the cleft in his chin, and his eyes were the color of a glacial lake. When she first met him, their combined heat combusted into the kind of relationship where there's just enough psychological tension to fuel wildly intense nocturnal grapplings that almost feel like love. "You're amazing, baby, even if it's just sex," he would sometimes whisper into her sweaty neck, then laugh before rolling away to sleep at the opposite end of the bed. She always laughed along with him, keeping it light. But after five months of passion, he informed her that, although he'd been unusually faithful (for him), monogamy was something he'd never done before and didn't really want; he smiled, moved by his own honesty. And maybe, just maybe, we shouldn't blame him for being surprised when she cried as if her heart was breaking.

Small Hands, Cold Feet

by Maggie Whitehead

Small hands pick at a thin paper gown intended to protect from disease and shame, yet only succeeding at one. Cold feet swing, hitting the metal plate that surrounds the bottom of the bench where I sit - breaking the silence with a sharp, intermittent percussion. Back aches from thirty minutes spent in this position - time enough to learn that you're gone, but not yet enough to digest your absence. Small hands make moves to constructively fill the silent space of time by pulling the paper gown tighter around my waist, fighting against the climate-controlled air that pricks at my skin until it finds its entrance, traveling down my veins and wrapping itself around the hard, secret knot forming deep inside my chest. The beat of my heart quickens under the weight of a realization: I loved you, little one; and although they tell me you've left - no doubt accurately assessed me for the mess I am and opted for an early check out – that I love you even still. But still... all that remains on this bench and in this gown is but one heart, small hands, cold feet, and the hollow place you left behind.

Vegetarian

by Tharuna Niranjan

I am constantly trying to impress upon my soon to be 6-year-old the merits of vegetarianism. The last time I broached this subject, about a year ago, he declared that he is a Lion; and that he usually eats antelopes, buffaloes, and wild boar, and only when he cannot find those, which is always the case these days *[sigh]*, he settles for chicken. The other day in the San Diego Zoo, he declared *[yes, its always a declaration with him]* that we *[me, him, the zoo and collectively the country]* need to bring home more gorillas from the African wild so we can save them from the bushmeat trade *[thanks to his newly acquired reading skills and voracious appetite for reading anything and everything, including the educational, conservation-tips-dispensing signboards at the zoo]*. Then I pounced upon my golden chance, I wasn't going to let go of the opportunity, and tried to pull him into a discussion about vegetarianism, about the fact that poor chickens are being killed to make butter chicken curry *[his favorite]* and that we should also try and save the chickens by becoming vegetarians. I was proud of my logical reasoning skills, sure that I have impressed upon him, by extending his own train of thoughts into the realm of animal rights and vegetarianism. He thought for a minute and then declared: "Mama, lets send the chickens to the African bush people and bring the gorillas into the zoo!"

Star-Crossed Lovers

by Ian Rochford

I guess it's my fault for falling in love because, straight away, I knew she wasn't any ordinary woman; with that strange, sexy accent and those amazing eyes, I knew she wasn't from around here. I guess you could call it a whirlwind romance since we met during a whirlwind, at a truck stop in the desert. First the wind swept me off my feet and then she did; actually, she grabbed my leg and held onto a petrol pump with the other arm. She sure was strong, because when the blow was over, just her, me and the pump were left. She was on vacation, traveling around the world and I was a drifter but, nonetheless, it was love at first sight so we had a registry wedding, and her trip became our honeymoon. After that, I went home with her to meet her folks and, well, don't get me wrong, they're nice people and all, but as I stand here in their golden palace looking out at those two purple suns in that green sky, I can't help feeling I wasn't given all the facts.

Precedent

by John Parke Davis

There is a country in the east where the laws grow in crystals, deep beneath the ground. The young lawyers are miners, and the elder, gem-cutters, they carve and polish the facets till the laws gleam just right. The judges are master gemologists, and whenever there is a conflict, the two sides will present him their most beautiful law-diamonds, and the judge will examine them through his loupe, turning them around and around and squinting to see the slightest flaws and imperfections. Only the most perfect laws survive, and in this way, the people of that Eastern nation are bedecked in the finest law-stones, and they sparkle like the sun. Around here, though, we have only dirt. Our laws work much the same way, but the results aren't nearly as pretty.

Lucky

by Megan Elliott

"This just isn't working," was what you said on the
last night, before you left. I threw an empty beer
bottle at the back of your head as you were walking
out the door. You were taking the stairs two at a time
and there was no looking back, but you still ducked
just before the bottle hit the wall ~ you were always
lucky like that. I had hoped that in loving you some
of that luck would rub off on me, but I guess that was
asking for too much. I still live in the apartment that
we shared together. Every day, I expect to see you
sitting on the stoop when I leave for work; every
evening when I return home I check the mail for a
postcard that never arrives.

Part 2

——————————

Ascent

Pandora's Box

by Juliana Perry

It's taken 15 years to figure out why I have been saving a handful of letters from my father, all of them signed *Love, Dad.* I sealed the correspondence away years ago in an archival plastic sleeve, more protected than my daughter's first artwork, secure in a box labeled "Important Documents." The letters have been boxed up through my twenties and hidden during my first marriage. In the midst of divorcing my abusive husband I discovered the box of letters and like Pandora, I knew better than to open it but I am a glutton for punishment. The outrage I harbor reading those words from a father to daughter is tempered with fear and loathing; it hangs on in the muck and mire of my past. As a mother I step carefully over the trip wires as I forge my own children's future free of abuse.

Under the Frying Pan

by Christen Buckler

The street corners are cold at night, and she's blinded by the oncoming headlights of the cars that may or may not belong to the local police department. All she has in her fridge at home is half a loaf of white bread and an oil-filled jar of imitation peanut butter. Her youngest sometimes watches as she gets dressed, admiring the eyeshadow and the false eyelashes, the trappings of such a glamorous lifestyle. Tonight is the coldest all month, and few cars cruise past her as she stomps her feet to keep warm and recites all the nursery rhymes she knows (the ones she'll coo to her children as their heavy eyelids close in exhaustion). Once she had a dream full of flames: her children witnessing her nighttime career and fire engulfing their tiny sweet faces - she watched them burn alive, but the only words she could scream were the ones belonging to her favorite little rhyme. *Ladybird, ladybird, fly away home, your house is on fire and your children all gone.*

Lessons from the Toolbag

by Lee Herman

Working as a remodel carpenter has probably taught me as much about people as any other people-watching experience has. When people can't afford to purchase the item they've selected from the grocery store, they simply put things back without trying to negotiate over price, the clerk's wages, or the overall cost of running a grocery store. They simply change their desires and ask for their new total, then pay the clerk like rational adults; however, when it comes to renovating their home, all the world and its ways are expected to change and to be seen through different eyes. Perfectly rational people lose all ability to reason, and you, the remodel carpenter, become personally responsible for constructing their dreams. I mean, turning their home into what they've always wanted, and "always wanted" usually goes back to childhood — the way they set up their dollhouse or the way they built their house out of Legos or Lincoln Logs (or a deck of cards, for that matter). And you're expected to do so on their budget and time schedule — unfortunately, we live in a world where budget comes before design.

Dirty Girl

by Dawn Corrigan

Once, when I was very young, one of the girls on the block was having a birthday party. Mom dressed me up for it, and I went outside with the other kids, but then there was a lull before it began. I started playing in the dirt by the curb, picking up handfuls and running them through my fingers. After a while some of the other girls noticed, and I guess by then I'd gotten myself and my party dress pretty dirty. A couple of the older girls decided to take care of things themselves, rather than getting a mom to do it. Though I disliked being dirty, I felt a rage that I was completely unable to articulate at the time, though I know the words now: How dare you clean me up?

The Plan

by Kerrin Piche Serna

Okay, here's how you do it. Listen carefully; I'm only going to go over this once. You go up to the man in the tweed jacket sitting on that pile of old tires and you tell him that you're part of the fire brigade, to which he'll have no response, but he'll hand you a dollar which will be dirty and crumpled and you can unravel it but don't smell it, whatever you do don't you dare smell that dollar. You take that dollar right over to the Ninety-Nine Cent store where you buy a tiny bottle of gin for the man – they're in the bin all the way in the back next to the blank video tapes – and when they give you your penny change (if they try to give you trouble about buying the tiny bottle of gin you tell them it's medicine for your mother, if it's the guy with the acne he'll chuckle at that and let you through) you take that penny and put it in the second - the second, mind you - gumball machine just inside the door, and it will spit out four gumballs because for some reason there's just something crazy wrong with that machine. If there are any red ones in the bunch I get them, otherwise it's two for you and two for me, fifty-fifty. Now go.

Numbers

by Andrew David King

Sometimes it seems like these fields stretch into eternity. If you stand facing the midday sun – lifting your eyes just enough so you have to squint – and stay still for a minute, you can feel like you're floating, almost hovering above the headstones. "Hmm," I say, looking down at the nearest grave marker, "only five words on this headstone, five words to stand for a life..." She looks at me a bit oddly before she says, meticulously, "If you only had five words to say that people would remember you by, maybe a lesson, maybe a memoir, what would they be?" I hardly consider this question for long before the words leap from my mouth, a spring of water in the desert of silence between us. "Time passes fast," I say, lifting my head towards the sun, my eyes beginning to squint, "don't blink."

Resolution

by *Peter Holm-Jensen*

The will falters yet again, so soon after being rebuilt;
the drinker awakes that night in a pool of guilt; the
farce continues. *O Subtle Visitor, O Night Magic. I
confess my will is broken; let me leave it on this altar I'm
building for you with shaking hands; give me yours.* Dawn
is born in trepidation. The dove is thrown over the
glistening water, flapping in panic. It remembers its
element, regains poise, and gives itself up to the
winds.

Husband Number One

by Stephanie Wright

Husband Number One – bless his heart – was the desperate choice of youthful desire to be rid of parents perceived to be overbearing. She imagined him to be the sure route to freedom without recognizing she merely traded one set of shackles for another. A wife at twenty-one, a mother at twenty-two, and a divorcée at twenty-five, she ran the gauntlet of sidelong looks and snide remarks, living in a run-down apartment she accessed via the rickety staircase crusted with dirt and eroding with rust where the handrail turned its ninety-degree corner at the landing. Some weeks, she fed the kid macaroni and cheese from a box two or three times if the rent was due or the child support check bounced. She went back to school at night, taking the kid with her if the babysitter didn't show, and the first Christmas was spent around a fluffy cedar with Husband-Number-Two-to-be. It was a shame she never enrolled in the course on decision-making.

Threefold Path

by Don Pizarro

Once again, I'm caught in the crossfire between Toni
and Evan during a Scrabble game. Toni tried to play
the word *tranny*, but Evan wouldn't have it because it
didn't exist in his ancient tattered dictionary. I backed
Toni since she actually is a tranny, and it is a real
word, and what's right is right. But Evan stuck to his
guns, holding that dictionary like it was a tablet
handed to him on Sinai. So I turned coat and
backed him because after all, rules are rules. It didn't
matter to me either way, really - I just wanted to play
my last two tiles to spell the word *zen*, which *was* in
the dictionary, for a triple-word score.

An Afternoon of Eggs

by Emma J. Lannie

Holly is smiling and talking to me and using her hands to make shapes of communication in the air above us. Every now and then, our eyes will catch on each other, and we hold this like an egg between us, until one of us puts it down gently and carries on with the words and the stories we are writing our afternoon into. Even when the air changes, when the din from the traffic becomes a loud hungry monster and the sun drops a bit heavier in the sky, we lie there with our ideas spinning lively between us, completely oblivious to everything else in the entire world. When the sky stops letting down so much light, Holly's arm brushes mine and with wide open eyes she says that we've been out here ages and where did all the time go? I let my arm fall against hers, emboldened by her own arm's proximity, and it feels like there are magnets in there, swishing around with the blood and the lymph. Holly makes no attempt to move away, to unglue her arm from mine, and I breathe slowly and keep my cool, even though I feel like my heart is about to pop.

At This Point

by Sophia Macris

At this point, two years later, I find him no longer an individual but rather a gestalt of representative elements. Peter Krause, the actor to whom he bears an uncanny resemblance, in a particular film from an Andre Dubus story about the disintegration of a relationship. The mock-heroic voice of Stephin Merritt, intoning a song titled "The Night You Can't Remember (The Night I Can't Forget)." An uncomfortable pause when shifting into reverse and letting out the clutch, the reminder of a driving lesson gone awry. He is only a definition, not really an object. And maybe that's all he ever was, a set of characteristics I found conveniently attractive, a person I really didn't understand at all.

Contact

by caccy46

They sat silently at the kitchen table, sipping their
morning coffee, each staring at nothing in particular,
trying to wake up. She looked at her daughter and
saw the sadness that lay beneath her sleepy eyes; and
in an attempt to connect, cautiously asked, "Any
plans for today, Sweetheart?" The young woman took
a deep breath and exhaled a loud, exasperated puff;
rolling her eyes, she growled, "Will you leave me
alone, Mother?"   Stung by the harshness of the
response, the mother sat quietly thinking and
carefully chose her words - "I love you and will always
be available to talk about your anger; but as of this
moment I have decided I will not tolerate your
contempt. I don't deserve it, and I think contempt
corrodes your soul." The arrow hit dead center as the
daughter erupted in tears and sobbed, "I'm so sorry,
Mommy" ~ a name she hadn't used since she was a
little girl.

Gone

by Sara Crowley

She said, "I always knew that he would leave one day, and he did." Then she opened the freezer drawer and pulled out zip lock bags, all neatly labeled in her tiny handwriting: FECES, SWEAT, BOGIES, SPERM, EYELASHES, HAIR (PUBIC), HAIR (ARMPIT), HAIR (HEAD), SKIN, NAILS, FLUFF. "I will make another one," she said. There was something chilling in her voice and I didn't doubt that she would. I made my excuses and left. I have not been back.

Six On My Mind

by Madam Z

Some people accuse me of being obsessed with Six, but I disagree and accuse them of sixual harassment. It's true that I often have sixy dreams, which sometimes involve same sex Six, or Six with animals, but that doesn't make me a Six offender, does it? And my favorite sixual fantasy involves me having Six on a desert island with six sexy men, but that doesn't mean I'm oversixed. I never had pre-marital Six, because Six hadn't even been invented way back then. I have had *extra*-marital Six, because hubby isn't interested in Six and I have to do *something* to relieve my sixual tension. He is, however, very interested in sex, so after we make love I sometimes sit at my desk and engage in post-coital Six, and that's the best Six of all.

Check Yourself

by Sherrie Pilkington

It's true, everyone knows I'm not exactly happy about how it all went down, but I'm not mad at her personally, so I tapped her on the shoulder, mustered a pleading expression and said, "Rebecca, I think you need to check yourself." She lowered her head, looked me straight in the eye and replied, "Oh *really*, I think maybe *you* need to check *yourself*." I tried again, "This is awkward enough, but seriously I'm trying to help you." She placed both hands on her hips and took a step closer to me, "What's truly awkward is that you're still mad you didn't get this award and you're trying to mess with my head before I go up there and give my acceptance speech." She ascended the stairs, confidently glided across the stage, grasped the extended microphone and turned to face the packed room allowing everyone to continuously receive glimpses of what I had noticed. *Zip your pants* shouldn't have been that hard to say, yet having not said it leaves me strangely satisfied.

Last Week was My Birthday

by Jennifer Moore

You didn't fall down the stairs and break your neck.
You didn't electrocute yourself on the dodgy toaster.
You didn't walk out in front of a speeding bus. I shut
my eyes and blew out the candles like everyone said.
Still nothing. So much for wishes.

Here Be Beasts

by Peter Wild

Here be beasts he said as the night drew in, the seven of us huddled together for warmth about the twitching flicker and snap of the campfire. There was something - something of the pirate and something of the ghost of a long-dead Confederate judge - in the way his eyes roved about us and we shivered like a huddle of conifers (or leastways *I* shivered and I'd pay good money that shiver passed like a Mexican wave along the spines and shoulder blades of my compatriots, the way we all took to looking around and smiling nervously as if we knew we were in for a treat of sorts, something devilish fine). Of course none of us had any inkling what that night had in store for us then. How could we? We were children, more or less. But I'll tell you this (and it just goes to show how wrong I was): when Rosie took my hand and squeezed, our two hands hidden beneath her casually discarded security blanky, I thought nothing bad could ever happen again.

Not Just a River in Egypt

by Jason Davis

The water rises around our ankles and shins, it floods our doorways, swamps our front porches, comes glistening and wet in dirt-flecked rolling rivulets down the basement stairs. The streets go fluid; highways become rivers, alleys become streams, and the day-to-day tracks of our lives submerge. We live in submarine suburbias where trips to the grocery store are triathlons, and every house has a dinghy or a pontoon moored to its personal dock; the stock of outboard motors soars. The city highrises transfigure into salt-stained pylons, barnacles braid the street signs, the homeless float or drown, and abyssal fish make new homes in our abandoned, silt-filled subway stations. Dolphins and catfish come into vogue and wealthy young women carry mudskippers in their designer, wet-to-wear purses. And the whole time the government man on TV says nothing has changed.

Ghost Image

by Brent Fisk

Gone. Even in the photographs you could tell he was
gone. Only the flashbulb put a shine in his eyes, and
the face he turned to those who approached was like
the open hand a politician offers in a crowd. From
his chair, fragments of sentences: words, questions
that made no sense. Wind moving leaves across the
parking lot, a rabbit dashing away from the sweep of
headlight beam, soft voices filtered through a wall.
When mother leaned in to kiss him goodbye, his
lucky guess, "You're my daughter," a whisper that
stayed with my mother like the ache of an old broken
bone.

Wisdom Teeth

by E.Y. Kwee

Reclining in the padded chair could have been any
trip to the dentist — except the dentist never tilted her
so far back in the chair so that her head was arched
towards the ground, and the dentist had never shot
her face so numb. "Scared?" he asks, and she replies,
"Yes," and he says, "A lot of people have had their
wisdom teeth removed this morning." The assistant
is holding a long tube of water and a long instrument
while the doctor sticks a black thing in the side of her
cheek to keep her mouth propped open — wait,
where's the laughing gas? But it's too late now
because the drill is coming in and the squeaking
sounds of cracking teeth indicate that it's too late
now to matter. Momentary terror rises like bile, and
then abates as she automatically suppresses it... now
he's trying to make conversation — like she's
supposed to respond — what the hell's he saying? If
only she had the laughing gas... and then he's lifting
out white bloody shards and vacuuming up the rest of
the millions of little pieces and what's left of her
tangible wisdom is gone.

Me, Myself, and a Pile of Magazines

by Jamie Boyt

When I was a boy, I found a stack of my dad's girlie magazines in the shed. The pictures were fascinating, and for reasons it wouldn't take me long to discover, I couldn't help going back for more. I'd never seen women like them, certainly not doing things like that, and the *stories!* Those images, the words, the memories, would stay with me for a very long time; have a profound effect on my young mind. And then, one day, they were gone, and my world was tipped upside down. Millie, from *Bra Busters, Volume 7, Issue 6*, wherever you are, I love you.

Irish Roulette

by Robert Prinsloo

Bang. Bang. Bang. Bang. Bang. Click.

Just Jump!

by Melody Gray

Sky diving or bungee jumping; they both scare the shit out of me but excite me at the same time; although, they feel like the right comparison to taking the risk of being in a relationship again and potentially having my heart ripped out vs. being single and lonely and trudging through the dating scene. My best friend likes the fact that I'm single; she says, "Just sleep with them and avoid the rest of the trouble;" she wants to live vicariously through me. It's all easy for her to say; she has her man next to her every night, warm, comforting, and yeah maybe a pain in the ass sometimes but at least he's there, though she does take him for granted. She's already jumped from her plane and her bridge and made a quick cushy landing, but isn't really happy where she is and wants to be back up at the high altitude with me. I want the landing, it's scary and lonely up here, not knowing what you're going to hit on the way down, always doubting that rush... will you pass out when your head hits the icy cold water below, trying to maneuver and avoid rocks and trees on the way down? Will the parachute really open once I step out from the plane, weightless, giving myself freely to the sky around me; am I letting the right person pass me by because I'm afraid to let myself jump, and instead

93

stand paralyzed on the bridge or the edge of the plane... one foot in, one out?

Perfect

by *Rob Winters*

The boy walked through the garden, only touching the grass when it was inevitable, striding forward with feet of silk and the grace of an angel. She stood under the tree with eyes as radiant as toxic waste and skin as smooth as cold metal. When she touched his hand, briefly, the time a bullet floats through time before it hits, he trembled and looked up at the tree. The pink blossoms floated through time in gravity defying elegance and with a distinct perfection reminiscent of the soul of a Japanese sword. And the boy wept, a single life-defining tear. For he realized he loved the blossoms and not her.

Rage Therapy

by Dark Icon

When Jones finished with them there was nothing left but blood and echoes, but he wasn't satisfied yet. He had already moved on to the next office when the voice started up again. *Jones, you have to abort this therapy session right now!* "Why?" *Because the drugs reacted... or rather, didn't react... to a peculiarity in your brain chemistry! This isn't a simulation, Jones... you've been awake for hours!*

The One Night

by Tim Horvath

This one night, though, he fancies himself a 6S
Grandmaster, setting up a sextet of computer
monitors in a row and facing off against them
simultaneously. One move, one sentence at a time,
then on to the next. On the first screen, the pawns
venture forth: a realist story inching out, something
about a dying fish and a broken relationship; on the
second the knights spring forth early as constellations
go to war in somewhat fantastical fashion; the third
(bishop-heavy) is three chums and bachelor exploits, a
voice-driven, Guinness-addled pukefest; on the
fourth, all pieces seem to move at once without a
single capture, a flip-book of digressions as words spill
tumultuously in a barrage of profligate verbiage; the
fifth, a sort of postmodern anecdote about painting
and circumstance and the relationship between art
and life, more chess puzzle than actual game; and
now on to the sixth screen - and the ticking timer
along with a desperation simply to fill the page makes
him fall back defensively into the cheap trick of
summarizing what's going on in the other five (+ free
bonus chess metaphor). Someone might slap the
postmodern tag on this one, too, but it's an old trick,
really, ancient as Scheherazade, who saw that daintily-
batted lashes would only keep her alive so long, and

97

thus tucked into the swirl of a thousand other stories the story of herself in the act of telling. She, of course, was fending off imminent throat-slash at the hands of an unforgiving, imperious caliph, whereas he lacks any such counterforce, thus is hardly like a Grandmaster after all. No, maybe he's more like the guy he occasionally recalls from his childhood who'd stand under the overpass of the Bronx River Parkway in Yonkers and whack a tennis ball again and again off the side of the highway; every so often, the rush of the traffic above must've sounded for all the world like the crowd at Wimbledon.

River Home for Eternity

by Rolland Love

A crow scolds me as I invade his stretch of the mighty Missouri river. I watch him fly away as I toss the ashes from an urn. The slate gray remains hover above the rippling water. Carried by a breeze they slowly drift downstream. I look toward the heavens as the ashes sink beneath the cold, icy water. My promise fulfilled, I wonder who will promise me?

Words Fall

by David Gianatasio

Words leap from the page. There they go, one by one: "irreconcilable," "division," "custody." They flutter and fly. Do you remember when Rachel was born, we... sorry, I know; yes I KNOW - I'll call you... well, I'd like to... I'll call... is that okay? Words form random patterns on the bleached linoleum tiles. Strange how they drift and die.

Loss

by Tara Lazar

She's in the closet grabbing dirty clothes, yanking
hangers, pulling towels off the shelves, wide-eyed and
frantic, so I know to back off. When she gets like
this, any comment can force her to attack; she'll use
whatever she can against you, and she doesn't care if
it's petty, or if it happened fifteen years ago, she
wants you to suffer along with her — she must bring
you down. I'm used to it; I know the next phase
involves throwing something breakable — crash and
destruction her climax. I sit on the bed and wait
until she comes to me with icy blue shards of
Waterford in her hands like frozen tears. "I can't
find her pillow, the little purple pillow that smelled
like her hair," she says, and I nod because it's all I can
do. She's all fury and fire yet I'm the one burning
inside.

Phineas Gage's Gauge

by Abigail Levin Tatake

Her brain was worn and moth-eaten and unraveling at the hippocampus, so she set to work knitting herself a new one. She cast 75 stitches onto circular needles but wasn't sure if that was right since her prefrontal cortex was so badly frayed and given to poor judgment. As she clanged the metal needles toward each other, her late grandmother's voice sang out through her growing temporal lobe, guiding her in three quarter time: "IN, wrap, slip; IN, wrap, slip; IN, wrap, slip..." The worsted weight cerebrum careened back and forth with each completed row, and soon the new specimen was rendered in booming magenta. As she bound off each new lobe stitch by stitch, she wept months of bridled agony, glee and wonder. Exhausted now, she unraveled her old brain, flung it toward the cat, and went out in search of some dinner.

Marriage Counseling: Perspective 1

by Jennifer Haddock

The therapist shifts in her chair, trying to bring the life back into her numb left leg. She practices the subtle art of clock monitoring: five more minutes of this damned tension, four more minutes of feeling helpless, three more minutes of the biting silence, two more minutes of growing chasms, one more minute until freedom. The husband begins to speak, but it is too late. The therapist turns her head all the way towards the clock as a signal to the couple. "I'm sorry, but your time is up." As she accepts the check and ushers them to the door, she thinks about the empty bed that awaits her at home.

Coping

by L.R. Cooper

The warm soft breeze was blowing her hair gently one way then another. The only sounds to be heard were the crescendo of waves crashing against the shoreline and just under that there was the call of the birds as they landed on the sand then ran to pick up their dinner with thin sharp beaks as the water receded. There was that relaxing quiet calm coming over her as she lay there on the sun-heated sand listening to the symphony of sounds. She started to feel the rhythm of the water in her body and wondered at the freedom of the birds as she sat there and contemplated the coming death of her mom. Since she was the only child there was no one else to turn to for the decisions that had to be made and each one broke her heart a little more. Thank whatever powers there be that she was close to the beach and it had this calming effect on her.

The Id Monster

by Robert Clay

Deep, deep down inside all of us, there is a one hundred million year old reptile waiting to get out. It's in there, somewhere, hiding in some forgotten corner of our labyrinthine DNA, biding its time, waiting for its day. Its savage coal black eyes stare across that vast chasm of time that separate us, murder in its heart, hunger and death its only reason. It may never emerge from that deep black pit, but it will always be there. Silent, deadly, and above all, patient. If you don't believe me, take a long cold hard look into a mirror.

Local Sheep Donate Wool

by Karl Winklmann

Harrisburg, November 21. In a heart-warming display of goodwill, the thirty-seven sheep on James McAlester's farm approached him on Tuesday with their wish to donate wool to a project that sends sweaters to orphans in Nepal. "I don't exactly know how they came up with this," McAlester said. He surmised that it had to do with the TV he keeps running in the barn. "The TV was stuck on the religion channel for a whole week," McAlester said. He has since turned it back to ESPN.

There Was a Time

by Alana Wilson

There was a time when I could feel the heat off of his body because we sat this close. I would watch him change gears while driving and imagine his outstretched fingers unintentionally brush my thigh. I could feel the currents of electricity deep to core of my body. I would sit in the passenger seat wishing that I were the kind of girl that would reach over to him and touch him in any way that I desired. The feelings of anticipation and yearning were so strong sitting inside that compact Honda. And now here we sit, his hand on my thigh, my hand playing with the hairs on the back of his head, comfortable in each other's presence; just once I would like to feel the way we did before we got married.

Why I'm Laughing

by Mercury

I'm laughing because you believed me when I said I forgave you. I'm laughing because you came here and didn't even take your shoes off, like you'd get to leave. I'm laughing because you actually took that drink. I'm laughing because you didn't know what was in it. I'm laughing because your vision is fading slowly, your head is pounding, you are staggering. I'm laughing because I'm the last thing you'll ever see.

Cold Turkey

by Teresa Tumminello Brader

I scour the neighborhood for our stolen turkey. I love his quizzical look and unsure eyes, which cause him to appear as if he isn't certain what life has in store for him. And it turns out he was right to worry, because who would have thought he'd be a victim in our upscale neighborhood. I see other turkeys in other front yards, but each has a different shape, different kinds of feathers and a happier expression than mine. Some of them even wear cartoonish costumes: I would never have done that to my turkey. I walk back to the front of our house where the Native American Indian girl and the pilgrim boy stand, as they do every November, smiles on their childlike faces and arms stretched toward each other, but to me the yard looks empty.

Bedtime Stories

by Linda Lowen

We have unacknowledged sleepovers of a sort, my
daughter and I - two females separated by a thirty-year
span of living - her unfolding experiences of 16 years,
my been-there, done-that 46 years of joy and regret.
This is how it happens: I'm sitting on the loveseat in
the family room, writing on my laptop, and she
wanders in, plops down on the couch, and ostensibly
clicks through nearly a hundred channels to find one
of 17 different daily reruns of *Scrubs*, one of her
favorite shows. You may think she's there to blow off
steam and watch TV, but it's more than that; and
though we don't always talk, it's a companionable
silence, and quite often small tidbits of gossip or
questions about live, love, and friendship surface,
since - like driving - it's sometimes easier to talk when
we don't make eye contact. The hour grows late and
she falls asleep; I stand up to tuck blankets around
her and then prowl the house before bedtime,
turning off lights and making sure doors are locked
before returning to my laptop and work. Somehow,
at some point, the TV gets turned off, my laptop
closes and is gently placed on the floor, I drift off -
curled up under my own blanket - and we sleep
perpendicular to each other, forming an *L* with our
bodies stretched out on the couch and loveseat

respectively. I remember when I first began to fall asleep with her sleeping next to me just after she was born, when she was still so small and yet so perfectly formed, with skin like soft velveteen and tiny exhaled breaths that smelled sweetly of milk; and though she is older, more restless in slumber, and has a few blemishes on that once-perfect skin, I still see that tiny baby in her tender, relaxed, sleeping face, and wonder if - when she goes away to college in two years - I'll be able to sneak into her room on nights when her roommate's not there and reenact these mother-daughter sleepovers, perhaps rising at dawn before she awakens to drive back to my own home with a contented smile on my face and a secret, silly yet bittersweet joy in my maternal heart.

Amber Alert

by Bryce Carlson

Two days ago, I was driving down Highway 55 and I noticed one of those disturbing amber alerts that read: BLUE HONDA SEDAN 4YQP821. My car is a black Honda sedan so it caught me off guard. It is my nature to always take serious note of this kind of thing because I've always wondered what would happen if I found the car. Of course, by the time I exited to venture home, I had seen nothing remotely close to the suspected vehicle. There was an unfamiliar car parked in my driveway when I arrived home and I pulled up behind it and read the license plate: 4YQP821 — and it was a blue Honda sedan. After pondering whom it could possibly be in the middle of he day, it dawned on me that my zany Uncle Leonard was in town for a visit.

Want

by Silvi Alcivar

Sometimes when I walk across bridges, I want to jump off. I don't want to die. I just want to jump. I want to feel the rush of wind and fall and life and death and breath escaping my body, or in fright and panic, holding itself in. Until I do jump, I'll never know which it is. Will I sigh myself into the air that's made me, or will I hold it, hold it, hold it all in?

On Longing and Her Leaving

by Joseph Grant

I have seen the Devil in many forms but none as beautiful as she. For she cast a spell upon my existence like no other and held me duty bound to her every whim or need, mind, body and soul. Now in the silence of the morning room, my body aches to feel her soft skin once more against mine, the silkiness of her abdomen, the rise and fall of her hip, the warm smell of her cocoa butter skin, her breath upon my chest, the luster of her dark, wavy hair that undulated in slow, yearly processions down toward her perfect waist where I would bury myself endlessly; making her moan and purr like the kitten she was when we were younger and first in love. The flowers that were given her are opportunely forgotten on the bureau and the dissipating heat of where she lay and the scent of last night's perfume all bear witness to the fact that she was once here only a short while ago, but this is irrelevant for in time, she will be flying hours away, but yet her essence still lingers. Strange how the distance between us grew until the one day we have become no more. It is the most dangerous thing for a man to get what he deserves and to attain what he so truly desires, for in time, it may ultimately break him in the way that lovers are broken, promises to lay cold and forgotten, it would be better to never have loved her at all, for all is torn asunder in the end and we to become you and me and descend we into our disparate, desultory abandon.

Getting Ahead for Myself

by Andrew Woodward

Our cause was lost, many of our kinsmen dead, and our Prince Charlie now on the run, but I could feel some satisfaction as I hefted the head of the British officer who ordered the cannons that took the life of many a brave and bonnie lad, even taking a moment to spit in his lifeless eyes. I found it curious that no one paid me any heed as I walked through our encampment, as surely my kinsmen would be glad to know I was alive, but none even looked up at me, let alone greeted me or offered me a dram of brandy. Those who looked my way gave me a look of sheer terror, crossed themselves, and shouted words of warding and salvation. My chief looked up at me and screamed also in terror; a mighty man who would jump into the pits of Hell to give Lucifer a black eye was now screaming and babbling like a sodie-heid madman. I was confused, but then, how was I to know that when he looked up at me, all he could see was a bloodied sword and the head of his enemy suspended in mid air. How was I to also know that I was dead too, killed by the cannons of my enemy whose head was still gripped in my hand that they couldn't see?

IKEA Prone

by Maura Campbell

Did you know IKEA is a four-letter word? The expletives explode as you find yourself bound in discarded shrink-wrap and littered with packing peanuts, counting small parts, squinting at directions and diagrams and making the walls blush after discovering you've just spent two hours assembling your new chair back-#$%*@-wards! A few choice words and hours later, you sit triumphantly on your new IKEA throne - congratulating yourself on a job well done. Then, an IKEA version of postpartum amnesia sets in. That was easy; we could really use another sofa. Now, where did I put my keys?

Go Give a Hug

by Saif Khan

When I cry because my mother cries, a connection is realized. Unbreakable like the five sticks of chewing gum stretched between my fingers and teeth, the connection wavers taut and loose; sometimes it's plucked like a guitar string, resonating immeasurable chords. Sounding off through grins and fits, this connection stays the same. A union or bond of different tastes, it melts the middle to create a common place. Embrace. *Embrace*, I say!

A Lesser Destiny

by Linda Courtland

The doctor said my tonsils were too swollen; he'd need to shoot me full of steroids. He slipped me a prescription and seven days later, I lit up my throat with a flashlight, looking for signs of progress. My tonsils modeled their finely-toned physiques, reveling in the spotlight. The little bodybuilders bragged to my adenoids about their newfound athletic prowess and dreamed of a future in professional sports. But later, when the euphoric effects of the medication had worn off, the fleshy organs spent long nights lamenting their documented steroid use. My tonsils will never play major league baseball.

Have You Slept in a Wigwam?

by Brian Steel

"Have You Slept in a Wigwam?" asked the weather-beaten wooden sign on the side of the road, advertising for The Wigwam Village, which consists of ten oversized concrete tee pees doubling as motel rooms and arranged in a semi-circle around the "Campsite," which is really nothing more than a gravel parking lot. The Wigwam Village had seen better days; specifically, the days before Interstate 40 carved a path of Days Inns and Motel 6's forty miles north of Holbroke. That night, I did sleep in a wigwam, but it wasn't until the morning that I realized the significance. Standing in the parking lot, smoking a cigarette, I saw the baby-blue '57 Chevy parked outside the front office, its hood shining brightly in the Arizona morning, its metallic trim reflecting the sun, and down by the wheel wells, the unmistakable creeping of encroaching brown rust. The café across the street was open, one solitary light shining on one solitary waitress who sat at the counter and dreamt of the Dairy Queen forty miles north. A plane, probably bound for L.A., roared overhead and that small, silver shard of metal cut a path through the top of my tee pee, leaving a perfect white scar against the blue sky of a new morning.

Part 3

—————————————

Cruising Altitude

Some Kind of Expert at Drowning

by Bob Jacobs

I once read an article on the Internet which suggested that a lot of people who drown (according to those who were subsequently revived, at any rate) spend their final moments feeling stupid, believing their loved ones will think them silly for getting into difficulties and drowning. I didn't want that to happen to me, to spend my last few moments before leaving this world feeling stupid. I figured I would want to spend those last moments in a classic rerun of my life flashing before my eyes: memories of my first love, my last love, scenes of natural splendor, moments of elation, feasts, naked romps, holding my newborn son, watching a total eclipse, the first moon landing, the restaurant scene from *When Harry Met Sally*, and so on. So I practiced in the bath, holding my breath for as long as I possibly could with my face submerged, training myself to replay my life in the thirty or so seconds (forty-odd on an empty stomach) for which I could prevent my lungs from bursting. I almost blew it once, I forgot to breathe, lost in the memory of a sexual encounter with an aunt when I was fifteen, but over a period of several months I became some kind of expert at drowning with just enough self-control to see the whole of my goddamn life flash before my eyes before the water rushes in.

So, here I am, trapped upside-down in this burning fucking car while my skin peels off, and all I can think of is how stupid I feel for wasting all that time in the frigging bath.

God Gives Us Free Will

by Margery Daw

Ruchl was raised in an Orthodox Jewish household, and spent her childhood reading the backs of food packages. She was only allowed Kosher, "consecrated," clean food, so her family had to make long trips to a special butcher shop for their meat; and crackers were only okay if they didn't have animal fat in them; and cheese had to be certified free of select disapproved enzymes. Passover was a whole other story - not only did her tradition forbid bread, it also forbade corn, rice, millet... and, as Ruchl discovered, *everything* contains corn syrup. Now that Ruchl - Rachel - runs her own household, she's dispensed with all that clean-consecrated-Kosher superstition. She treats herself to long trips to special stores - Whole Foods, Trader Joe's - with foods that reflect her personal values and preferences: grass-fed, free-range, organic meats; crackers with no saturated or trans fats; cheese certified free of recombinant bovine growth hormone. She continues to read labels, though, because corn syrup is in *everything*.

The Last Supper

by Montgomery Maxton

This is the steak dinner where everything falls apart
because what we have between us on the table is too
tender; what we have between us at hand is too raw.
The waiter that sips my goblet and you shout at. The
chefs refusal to cook my meat medium well. The lady
who checked my bag and said there were too many
immigrants in America. This is where you paid two
hundred dollars to shoot yourself in the foot and me
in the hand. A bad aim changes the world just as
much as a good aim; the bullet is still the same, the
blood is still lost.

Graduation Goodbye

by Raquel Christie

For those I have lost over these four years. For Michelle McCall, my dear high school friend, who died in childbirth; who dies in childbirth anymore? Sweet, sparkly Michelle, bubbly, brown curly Michelle, glittery black eyes with tiny iridescent stars in them, stars like Michelle, who played the flute like an angel and spoke with big, archaic words that she brought back to life and who squeaked when she laughed, like a baby, like the baby she left college to bring into this world, the baby who swiftly took her out of it. For Doug, who I hardly knew but who gave me his room when I didn't have one, the room with the odd smell and the bright yellow Curious George Poster - "Show Me The Monkey!" it said - and I thanked him and never saw him again. For my beautiful, tall, lean Aunt Vicky, who was fiery and platinum blonde and brilliant, and Uncle John, who was determined, strong, hard-willed, sometimes wrong-willed, but always very kind - and for the children they left behind, my cousins, the strongest people in the world, who are making something of themselves in a town where most don't. For my Grandpa Bill: my memories of him are faint but they are of a man who, if not popular, was always himself, and would never hurt a fly or his family; a respectful rebel - he's probably smoking in Heaven, playing poker with God.

How We (Almost) Killed a Toddler

by Sarah Flick

Karen and I must have been second-graders on that sunny morning when all the grownups went out, leaving us to baby-sit her 3-year old cousin, David. We gave him lots of candy yet I felt uneasy watching him lie on the carpet working his jaws up and down, because it just didn't seem right. Suddenly, as if in response to my thoughts, the little guy produced a gargling, gagging noise followed by alarming silence; he sat up, opened his mouth, and made retching motions but no sound - or candy - came out. He rapidly turned purple as I stared in horror, while Karen ran to get an older sister from the other end of that very large house. Sister Julie, fortunately, proved to be an unusually resourceful 11-year old, having raised herself and several dogs without much supervision. She arrived, held David upside down by his feet, and shook briskly until he vomited up gummy-bears and finally cried - sweet, sweet sound.

Babies and Drugs

by Shaindel Beers

Walking past the baby supply aisle of Bi-Mart, she wonders if anyone else has ever thought about how babies and drugs just seem to go together, and she starts listing other items that go together — macaroni and cheese, bacon and eggs, babies and drugs — it is a mantra that carries her through the store. In high school, you'd go to someone's house to baby-sit, and, inevitably, your friends would come over, and you'd end up drinking or smoking pot, and it was hard to believe that babysitting had been the reason for the whole outing in the first place; the kids were just your passkey into a new and exciting world of someone else's liquor cabinet and porn stash. And then, when one of your friends got pregnant and had a baby, it was always a stoner. Girls "with potential" got abortions; it even seemed that college applications should have a blank to list your abortions to prove that you really wanted to go to college, you really wanted to succeed; it was the only thing that mattered. But now, suddenly, the world has gone crazy — everyone is having babies — even people you're pretty sure aren't constantly stoned — your doctor, the lawyers who live next door. But then, you think about prescription drugs, and it all makes sense

— yes — they're just like you — only they're doing it legally.

A Homecoming

by Joseph Grant

At night the war would come back to Lieutenant Paul Hutchins in the visage of horrific nightmares, close echoes of a war he thought he had put behind him (readjusting to civilian life had been tougher than he ever imagined, for the silences became as loud as the war had, everyone was a suicide bomber in his eyes and the shadows crept up on him, ready to assail him at every peaceful moment). One would think that seeing his family and being home again would return him to tranquility and order, but it took the same sort of adjustment, as his cold and distant father had not changed, he had just aged and his mother, obstreperous as always, did not age, but that was due more to the miracle of Botox and subtle plastic surgery procedures than to clean and stress-free living and his sister was still engaged to that cholo-wannabe loser, trapped in a relationship that was never going anywhere, much to his mother's derision, his father again, typically distant and removed. With good intentions, his girlfriend, Heather, had planned an off-the-chain homecoming party for him, despite the fact that he told her in no uncertain terms he was in no mood mentally to the idea of being lauded as a hero for just getting wounded and that he had already been home for almost a month and that the only heroes of the war came home in a body bag or not at all. These thought raced through his mind as he sat at his own welcome home party, a party he did not care to be at and decided the only way to endure the endless handshakes and phony backslaps of neighbors who could not stand him before he shipped out, was to get rip-roaring drunk. As he hobbled around the party on his crutches, he made the best of it that he could for Heather's sake, but before long, he became more and more unsteady and noticeably drunk, a few times being pulled into the kitchen by his pushy and officious mother to whom of course, appearances were everything. The last straw came when Heather's thug ex showed up at the party and Paul, feeling no pain, greeted him coldly and then got into a verbal war of words that escalated into fists in front of the horrified guests, which in turn made Paul swing his crutches, finally ending with the spray of gunfire that sent guests fleeing and took Lieutenant Paul Hutchins's life not on some indecipherable battlefield in Iraq but in the comfort of the his own American backyard.

Dancing

by E.Y. Kwee

It's red and white and GREEN, the swirling
embroidered colors on the swirling dresses of the girls
in the Mexican hat dance routine; the boys are in
black and white and other colors and it suits them,
though not as well as the radiant expression to one
girl's face as she shuffles skillfully, taps masterfully,
and dips effulgently. The crowd is thick, maybe 10
people deep, so people are standing on the benches
near the back to have a better view — in the midst of
the dancing — *the glorious dancing!* — one dancer might
have stopped to wonder what a spectator was
thinking as they gazed upon the spectacle of four or
five perfectly in sync couples, whirling in perfect
symmetry to the canned but exhilarating music. She
might think of how a spectator might ponder upon
seeing such boys the same age as the spectator herself,
boys that are moving with grace, poise, and
possession such that she's never imagined compared
to the cowardly, juvenile boys at school; perhaps the
spectator would ponder upon the smile on her face,
whether it was fake or not; perhaps the spectator
would ponder the meaning of life as the dropping
temperature drew the warmth from her cheeks,
leaving behind a satisfying numbing coldness;
perhaps the spectator would think upon her last love,

and the bruises he had left, trampling his way clumsily out of her heart, only to steal back in, as a ghost, to prolong the agony of the bruises. But the dancer is caught up in the passion and fire and fury of dancing, a release from reality and her own heartache – into the music for a little while, anyway. And the spectator might wish she had that kind of skill, even though she knows that her clumsy feet would probably dance their clumsy way right to the hospital if she attempted such a feat, or she might be wishing that she was fluent in Spanish, or that she could take a trip to Mexico. All this a spectator might be wondering, but who would ever know?

Still Good

by Monica McFawn

One day Froggy Dagnet showed me his masterpiece and taught me his methods. "They're usually all curled up and sort of hidden in the grass by where the road ends so you have to look down for one that's still shiny and doesn't look broke. Here's a good one 'cause it's green and big and isn't broke so now we take it to the stream and wash it out. You gotta turn it inside out and swish it around real good and maybe put your hand in it to get it stretchy so it hangs better." Froggy trusted me with the job of stretching and drying so I put my hand in it and spread my fingers as we walked to what he called his "Magic Bounty Tree," a big tree outfitted in about a hundred used prophylactics, some of them pulled over big branches, straining so they looked like squeaky webs, some of them filled with pinecones and rocks to help them hang low, some simply tossed up as high as Froggy could throw and these settled on the high branches like little angel stockings snagged off during a low flight. It was an awesome sight and I was as puzzled as Froggy when he said he didn't understand why people threw them out when they were still good.

Late

by Barry Graham

I would have gotten there sooner but I stopped in front of the Tropicana and paid $260 to a prostitute so I could stick it in her ass. She had clean white teeth and no needle marks and she looked Mexican, but all Latinas look Mexican if you're white. There were small black hairs all over the inside of her ass crack and small red bumps that could have been crab bites or scabies or regular old pimples if I was lucky. Her panties were black and unflattering; she was gorgeous. I pretended she'd been a whore from Venezuela since she was twelve and it made me come faster. She asked me to pull out but I didn't – who has time to pull out when they're late for Christmas dinner?

My But

by Steve Talbert

I love to show my but when I write, but I don't worry about breaking any decency laws. When I expose my but, I'm not actually mooning anyone. The "but" I reference is a part of speech — a conjunction — not a misspelled body part. For me, my but is indispensable, probably one of the most essential tools in my literary arsenal. I like to use my but in the first sentence of an article because I can juxtapose opposing information against a declarative statement. Sometimes, though, my but is buried deep in an article, but it's usually there somewhere.

The Gulch

by Peter Wild

It wasn't revenge driving him on, hand over hand, fist over fist 'neath the blistering noon day sun and it wasn't the small scrap of Leviticus Oyster'd torn out of his King James Bible (*whatsoever goes upon the earth and whatsoever goeth upon all four or whatsoever hath more feet among all creeping things that creep upon the earth them ye shall not eat for they are an abomination*) that somehow or other he'd managed to hang on to even when they were beating him with their pistols and feet and fists. It wasn't the pleasure he'd seen in their faces as they tossed him, battered, broken and bleeding from his eyes and his ears and his nose, all the way to the bottom of the Gulch and it wasn't the sound they'd made, the seven of them, Oyster and his men, the town counselors, chuckling like a freshwater spring as they rode away, all the way back to Carson City, fifteen miles or more from this blasted spot, damn 'em all to Hell. It wasn't the pain, the way his eyes throbbed and his knees buckled beneath him and the way his desiccated throat seemed to scratch every time he swallowed like a sheep snagged on a barb wire fence, and it wasn't the terror, the terror that seemed to reach its hairy arm in his mouth and down his throat the first time he had to climb over a dead body, the Gulch being full of the recently dead and the long dead, skin and sun-bleached bones all mingling together, so many hooks struggling to hold him down, all those dead bodies wanting him to join 'em, join 'em, join 'em for the long afternoon of the purgatorial soul. It wasn't any of these things that compelled him to claw at the sand, to scrabble and clamber up the sides of the Gulch like no man before him, the gut wound roaring hungrily in his belly, the blood spilling out through his sticky fingers, the noon day sun scorchifying and scorchifying and him, bleary-eyed, exhausted, less a man than a hate-filled hollow, taking a step and a step and a step, measuring out his intent in tea-spoon steps. What kept him going was the glimmer of unease he'd caught at the last moment in Liv's eyes, his Liv, as she stared out through the swinging saloon doors, the glimmer of unease that told him she'd known all along, or worse, was involved or at least knew what was coming, had betrayed him, even after all he'd done for her. Oyster and his men would get theirs alright, he knew that, was positively looking forward to plugging every single one of those sick sons a bitches but it wouldn't be over, not truly over, until he had Liv down on her hands and knees with the still warm barrel of his gun in her mouth, the tears running freely from her beautiful blue eyes and the snot bubbling up from that perfect little nose, and her, doing her best to say Sorry, her saying Sorry like she meant it, like as if Sorry could mend all of the things she'd done and not knowing that Sorry would be the last word she'd ever speak, on this planet or any other.

Sara Doesn't Wear Green Anymore

by Alun Williams

Sara began to sob quietly as her assailant in the Richard Nixon mask quietly unbuttoned her sodden trousers and pants and carried them into the kitchen. She heard the soft click and gentle hum of the washing machine and then he returned. "I've put them on a low temperature wash," he said, "so the colors won't run." She wondered stupidly if she should thank the man for his kindness but she felt ashamed that fear had made her wet herself. "You should never wear green because it's not you." Sara thought about this all the while as the guy in the Richard Nixon mask ran his hands over her body and decided she would never wear green again.

The Space Between Three Dots

by Victor S. Smith

There is this convention that says if I put down three periods, side by side, on paper it represents words that aren't said. So when you see them in a letter... it isn't a dramatic pause meant to elicit a response from you, it is where I am storing all the information that is too hard to say, or write, out loud. What better place to place the words, "I love you beyond comprehension," or, "When I wake up I want to be able to spend all day next to you in bed?" Because when you really think about it, we don't know each other that well. We had a chance meeting on the street and then one more through a friend of friend, and it might seem a little odd for me to be spilling out the contents of love-sick mind on the page. The ellipses take care of that; they help me to keep it friendly when what I really want to say is...

Fussy Eater

by Jennifer Moore

After the unfortunate incident in the pig shed she announced she was turning vegetarian. They did their best to humor her - feeding her up with extra portions of buttered potato and mountains of grated cheese on everything. With any luck, they thought, it was just a passing phrase. When she heard the cows bellowing in the fields, their bloated udders dragging on the grass beneath them, she said she was giving up milk. They bit their lips, said nothing, fearing for her brittle bones as they piled dry potatoes high on to her plate. The day she gave up potatoes, they sat down and wept.

Welcome to Arizona

by Nicole Ross

"I'm sad," I confessed, "about everything." "I know honey, I'm sad too," he said, "for you and Jack, for me and your mother, for break ups in general... but I mean look at us, we're at rock bottom; the way I see it, the only way to go from here is up." I nodded, although I was pretty sure that in order to be considered rock bottom, the situation had to involve a suicide attempt, or at least a lot of drugs. I hadn't gotten to that point yet, and hopefully, neither had my father. The irony of it all didn't escape me though, that my 71-year-old father and I were both in this new city, trying to get over our heartbreaks together. We didn't know how to do this, so we went with the next best thing: pretending to start a normal day by eating Honey Nut Cheerios and talking about the unbearable heat and the plethora of cacti.

Euthanasia

by Cate Stevens-Davis

The injection the veterinarian brings with him is
colored hot pink and it glows against the gray
landscape of the farm, like a bad 80's music video.
She thinks of it as a final indignity that the big horse
is brought to his knees by such a thing. His sweating
flanks heave, slacken, collapse finally onto the snow,
churned and muddied by his thrashing, unsteady
hooves. She strokes the soft neck, twining her fingers
in the coarse black mane, presses her salted lips to the
soft space above his eyes, ducking back to avoid the
swing of his confused head. Underneath his long
winter hair, the heartbeats – skips – slows – stops,
muscles twitch and relax, tiny tics up and down his
long legs before – nothing. She watches the man
with the truck, watches thick chains slung around the
animal's ankles, watches the heavy head dragged out
the gate, eyes open and gazing at the pregnant sky,
rolling in prayer or frustration.

Trading Up

by Rod Drake

I saw her in a Starbucks in the financial district, laughing and gently rubbing the hand of her apparently new boyfriend, a real sugar daddy from the expensive and mature look of him. That was not surprising, since Lola was always calculating in every move she made, even romantic ones. She played to win, and win big, so it wasn't that surprising that Lola left me when my once-promising literary career took a nosedive. She glanced my way several times across the crowded, noisy coffeehouse before recognizing me and then weighed her options in ignoring or acknowledging me. Eventually some shrewd purpose occurred to her, and Lola smiled dazzlingly at me, waving me excitedly over to her table, probably to impress her new boyfriend that she knew a published author. But before she could introduce me to her companion, who hadn't seen me yet, I cut in with "Hi Dad."

Being Black in America

by Darrick H. Scruggs

I grew up in a tough neighborhood where the use of illicit drugs was rampant. Our role models were the neighborhood drug dealers and the cool but otherwise worthless elders that littered the streets. These characters hung out aimlessly. They puffed on cigarettes and they came up with cool names for all of the kids in the neighborhood. In short, these ne'er-do-wells were local celebrities, but for all the wrong reasons. Still, for kids it often seems cool to have a slick sounding nickname and to be associated with someone who at least appears to be well respected in the neighborhood.

The Exposed

by T.J. McIntyre

She cried out into the icy night; the ghost of her breath rose in the cold sky as she exhaled her grief. Her long lost baby remained silent, hidden beneath the stout shrubbery, beneath a layer of snow, intertwined in the roots, undergoing a slow decomposition in the ice-hardened earth. "How could you?" they all asked, to which she had no reply, just an all-consuming regret, a gaping maw chewing away the rotting remnants of her once fertile womb. She had explained how the child was different, there was a problem, but they all saw the body and found it to be whole and without defect. Cast from the village she cried for her baby, and for the loss of the family she could have known if things were different. The ghost of her baby taunted her with silence as she joined the permafrost.

New Year's Wishes

by Diane Brady

I've given up on traditional New Year's "Resolutions" because they usually don't last more than a week. Instead, I'm going for New Year's "Wishes." *Peace On Earth* – a great idea if it weren't for the power-hungry greed of most world leaders and conflicts between religious groups who believe their spirituality is the only act on the planet. *Cures for AIDS, Cancer and Assorted Diseases* – this might be tough because the pharmaceutical companies would never survive if Americans weren't spending large chunks of their income on medicines and treatments. *Top Quality Education for Every Child* – imagine kids participating in class and studying at home instead of playing video games, and when too many varsity football players break the rules, the school actually canceling the Homecoming Game. Since the chances of these "Wishes" ever coming true are remote, I'm going for something with better odds like winning the $100 million Powerball Jackpot, having great sex all day and night or waking up New Year's Day without a hangover.

The Man

by L.R. Cooper

The screeching of the tires and the blasting of the
horn came to a sudden stop as the car slammed into
him with a vicious jolt. His body went flying into the
air and later onlookers said that it reminded them of
one of those acrobatic acts that you see in the circus,
the one where people go tumbling end over end
keeping your heart in your throat and your breath in
your chest as you watch. He flew into the air with
an amazing amount of elegance, doing cartwheels in
the air, one, two, then three times finally falling
towards the road head down. The woman standing
mesmerized nearest to where he was going to land
said that the most amazing thing happened when he
got near the curb on the other side of the street.
Apparently he twisted in the air landing on his feet
with a thud that she felt in her own heels, looked at
her and fell backwards sitting down with another
thud that wasn't as bone rattling as the first but still
managed to push all the air out of his lungs with a
loud groan. The other people on the street got to
him and were surprised to see him up and walking
away without the slightest sign of a limp and
mumbling to himself what sounded like "Not again,
not again."

When I Saw Her

by Silvi Alcivar

I was in the grocery store, choosing large brown eggs
over white ones, when I saw her sniffing a wet bunch
of parsley, trying to decipher whether or not it was
cilantro. She plucked a small sprig between her long
fingers with unpolished nails and without looking to
see if someone was looking, she placed the morsel on
her tongue, then sighed — as if to say tasting didn't
help — and laughed a little to herself, the way you do
when you think you're alone. "Cilantro," she said,
placing the herb into a clear plastic bag which she
closed with a loose knot then tucked neatly into the
plastic basket she held in the crook of her arm. I
watched her move through the produce a moment
more. She sniffed a pepper, squeezed a cantaloupe,
and stood watching the automatic mist pass over
green onions before she went back to the herbs and
tasted them again. I decided to leave her then, as she
stood laughing to herself amongst the parsley she
thought was cilantro.

Sea Legs

by John Parke Davis

Back on land, the air cannot hold my weight. I feel gravity's drag on every inch, every muscle, and pray it will go away, pop me up like a softball high into the sky where I can catch a thermal and ride the whole world round. My fingers, ozymandian pillars of stone, crumble off my body into piles of rubble, and I dare not look down to see where they have fallen for fear that my head will follow suit. Ants will play in my ruins, lead guided tours on a daily basis to the tip of my nose, they will think the rolls of fat on my belly are the natural contours of the earth and run and play across them until my bones are declared a historic monument; the Man Who Fell to Pieces. None of this happens. Instead, I stand on the shore and watch the water, silently swaying to the motion of the waves trapped in my ears.

Exposure

by caccy46

It was an awkward way for Maya to learn Richard was cheating on her the first day back from her vacation; she saw Sue, the law firm's know-all, see-all, tell-all indiscreet gossip - her non-stop chatter about all the news since Maya had been away included, "I didn't know you and Richard stopped dating; I met his new girlfriend, Janice, at the firm's dinner - she's cute, and they were all over each other." Trying to absorb the information, Maya's head throbbed while remaining focused on Sue's diatribe - allowing no sign of her inner havoc, she continued preparing her coffee. Over drinks several weeks ago, introducing Janice, her dearest and most trusted friend, to Richard, her new lover, was natural and fun, thinking they'd have lots to talk about; Janice, newly separated and in desperate need of advice and Richard, a divorce attorney at the firm. Shock drove her directly to Richard's office to confront him with her information; hoping for a reasonable explanation, she sat across from him and stared at a painting hanging on his wall of a super realistic ripened tomato, sliced open, exposing its luscious, juicy center. Richard, disarmed by the visit and at a loss of his usual articulate composure, fumbled his way through an explanation of how it happened; but was incapable of

153

understanding it was the deceit that crushed Maya. She looked at his face and spoke words that still haunt her: "How very appropriate that this painting should belong to you; it's a portrait epitomizing what you are - raw, exposed, and in the process of rotting."

Barren

by Teresa Tumminello Brader

Angela halts atop the levee, easily spotting the lot two blocks away where a friend's home once stood. The gap reminds her of a missing tooth, the gum raw and exposed. Rushing waters from the broken levee ripped the house off its foundation and pulled it away from its front porch steps. When Angela and her husband arrived to help Laura scavenge for salvageable items, they found a snow globe of New York resting in a corner of the porch. No one knew where it had come from. The concrete steps alone remain, awaiting visitors to cross a threshold into nowhere.

Late to the Party

by Jamie Boyt

I've always had a problem with timekeeping, ever since I was a lad; late for school, late for college, late for work, you get the idea. I'll never forget Jenny, and the Christmas party at the local hockey club, around the time of my 18th birthday. We'd only met the night before but she'd looked fantastic, and kissing her was awesome, so we had agreed to meet at the party at 8pm. When I eventually turned up twenty-five minutes late, she already had her tongue down some other bloke's throat. You'd think I would have been disappointed, and to begin with, I really was. Word is, though, he dumped her after just a few days, and spent the next few weeks trying to get rid of the genital warts she'd given him for Christmas.

Flip of the Coin

by Melody Gray

It was a flip of the coin when we were born, which one of us would spend the next few weeks in that heated bed with the lights that would cause the blindness, unknown at the time of course. You were chosen, but I would take care of you, because we spent the first six months of our existence together before anyone even knew who we were, our time as one sharing things we don't even know now. I was your eyes and you depended on me, sometimes too much for a child who just wanted to play and not be a mother; and I ran, wanting you to follow but you hit the wall, those little rocks on the house making your head bleed, it took me years to be able to forgive myself for running from you. When I walked to school to learn to read and write you flew on a plane, far away, to learn to read with your fingers, but you never learned because other bad things happened there that took you even further away in your mind than that plane could have ever taken you away from me. Where are you now, I've worried; waking up in the night afraid and wondering if you are hurt, scared, or lonely like me. We will always be as one, but I'm terrified that one day, again with that flip of a coin you will be taken from me on those lonely streets that you walk; will I know deep within my

heart that you are gone, before I even hear the words,
leaving me as only part of a person?

Untitled #2

by Michael Lipkowitz

Everything just became a dull shade of life, a dull shade of beauty, the same way I saw it in my dreams. The dreams where we'd climb the tallest trees, the tallest peaks; as we'd wipe the crisp silver snow from our numb foreheads, we'd look at the distant expanse that covered us and feel it. It was something strong, something overpowering; it was a sense of feeling, or the absence of feeling, or the appreciation of a beautiful emptiness within us. And our emptiness was everywhere, our emptiness was symphonic. We'd admire the impossibility of the mountains that surrounded us, the ridiculous majesty of it all. We'd feel the cosmic music shake the jade from our bones, the music of a thousand clouds and a million snowbirds, in chorus as one - this disjointed tune, this broken symphony that, in its infinite beauty, kills us with its sighing glory.

Manhole

by Dawn Corrigan

Today I saw two fire engines, and a man emerging from a hole in the ground. Two other men were there to pull him out. "Sorry," he said, as he handed one his walkie-talkie. Then they rolled the manhole cover over the hole. My first exposure to manhole covers was watching the children's TV show *Sesame Street*, where they made much of them. I always thought they looked like something good to eat, like the cookie part of an Oreo.

Marriage Counseling: Perspective 2

by Jennifer Haddock

The thick silence hangs a moment past comfortable before the man breaks in with, "All I know is that we don't have sex anymore. After ten years, where did the sex go?" He looks over at his wife as her right hand rolls the gold band back and forth across her left finger. He makes quick eye contact with her, and the emptiness there startles him. The man hears the therapist say something about their time being up. He wants to say everything at this point, but he says nothing.

How to Make Friends with Robots

by Steve Himmer

The first time the robots surprised me, and were able to make off with most of my stuff. The second time I was expecting them and not only did I get back my own stuff but I was also able to take some of the robots' stuff. The third time the robots expected me to expect them and tricked me out of my original stuff, their stuff I'd taken, and the new stuff I'd bought to replace the stuff they had stolen before. The fourth time the robots came, I grabbed as much of their stuff as I could but they grabbed more of my stuff, too. When the robots came for a fifth time, we all realized we were enjoying our get-togethers so much that we had a potluck instead of a raid. The sixth time the robots won't come because they've invited me back to their place, where I'm totally going to steal all their stuff because I think the robots will respect that.

In the Can

by Patricia J. Hale

One shot was all it took. I was ready for more, had plenty of bullets, lots of time, no qualms about a future prison sentence. I'd already killed someone that same afternoon, so it was a freebie. See, the robbery went wrong, as I told her it would, but she had to be stupid and insist on her way like she always did. It was on the convenience store security camera, no doubt about it, but she's managed to get me to knee-jerk to her barked order to shoot the clerk and he's dead now. Juries don't understand how you're forced into it, how you've got to just act, the idiots presume you can just sit and calmly consider your actions like some slow motion movie, but you can't, you have to just do it, you have to look at them straight on and watch them fall, watch them hit the ground, so I guess it was like a beautiful action movie, you see it in your mind in slow motion.

Every Woman is an Excuse to Drink

by Nathan Tyree

Yardley believed that every woman was an excuse to drink. At sixteen Helen had introduced him to strawberry wine in screw top bottles gulped in the back seat of his rust specked Impala. When he was twenty Suzy drove him to Wild Turkey diluted with cola in his dorm room on long nights when all he could do was weep. Twenty-four years old and abandoned by Colleen, whom he had planned to marry, Yardley had taken a week off work to settle into small barrel bourbons. Cindy had liked it that he drank Scotch and water, which she saw as the drink of a cultured gentleman. When she left him, he left the scotch behind and moved on to Vodka.

You're Reading This Title

by Bryce Carlson

Yes, you're reading this short exposé in order to see what I might be able to say in just six sentences. The first sentence caught you off guard because it perfectly described what you are doing at present, as does the current one you're reading, but alas, the title's meaning takes shape and becomes overwhelmingly clear. You're not scared, at least not yet, just interested, which is exactly how I planned this. You read this sentence wondering exactly how I could have "planned this" and what it is exactly that I have planned (let's just say that by the time you finish this parenthetical, I will be eighteen steps closer than I was when you started this sentence). "How is this working?" you ask yourself in your head, pondering how these words, printed on a page in *Six Sentences, Volume 1*, are able to describe exactly what is occurring in your life right now with such uncanny precision — you fight the fear, failing to notice that your breathing habits have changed from when you first started reading, and you convince yourself that this is just six sentences of nonsense but as I tell you, yet again, precisely what you are thinking, you speed through this last clause right here to see what awaits in the last sentence. As MuCh As YoU WaNt To FlY tHrOuGh ThIs SeNtEnCe, you are SLOWED down

by the AwKwArD fLuCtUaTiOnS in Letter case
(especially the word fluctuations), which I purposely
did to draw this out, but now you start to take your
time and read how I suggest that once you finish with
the final period, you pull yourself away from this
book and look behind you to see the person who's
been watching this whole time in order to give you a
remarkably fresh six sentences that, at this point, have
you filled with questions and an inkling of terror —
you finish this sentence.

The Lie

by Sara Crowley

He asked me if he was going to die and I told him that we all die sometime, but not yet, not now. His face was pale against the hospital pillow, the smudges under his eyes dark, as I explained that we die when our bodies are old and used up. I told him that children don't die because I didn't want him to be afraid. How many lies did I tell over all? Father Christmas, the Easter bunny, the tooth fairy, you're not going to die. I hope that he can forgive me.

My Mom Might Be a Little Bit Racist

by Eric Spitznagel

Last summer, I got into a heated disagreement with my mother about whether Native Americans should be called Indians. "But they're not from India," I reminded her, "they were native to North America long before we-" She cut me off with a groan. "Yeah, yeah, I know," she said, "and then they made a bad deal and lost their real estate, so boo-hoo for them. Maybe next time they should read the fine print." Four years of a liberal arts education, where I had so much PC rhetoric pumped into my system that it took several years before I felt comfortable dating a woman who shaved her armpits and didn't resemble Edie Brickell, and I had no response to her wildly inappropriate comment besides, "That is so unfair."

The Harvest

by Tara Lazar

Good apple pies are a considerable part of our domestic happiness, wrote Jane Austen; so inspired, we hike to the orchard in the early October morning, our fleece jackets and brisk pace keeping us warm despite the chill. Streams of sunlight escape around the trees, the limbs and leaves in shadow, like fragile silhouettes in a yellow sky. He offers his hand, but I duck under the canopy of trees to discover golden and crimson orbs peeking out in unexpected places, unwilling to announce autumn's climax and the inescapable descent into winter. Should we capture them to our basket and reward ourselves with a crisp bite, once again savoring the taste of beauty? As the sun climbs higher, swirls of our breath rise to the clouds. We reach for the cool, smooth skin of the fruit, twist gently, and hold Austen's promise in our hands.

Can't Sleep... Clowns Will Eat Me

by Adam J. Whitlatch

Can't sleep... clowns will eat me. I know they will, because their breath reeks of stale popcorn, moldy cotton candy, and children's toes; I could smell it when that one at the circus gave me the balloon today. I hate those fake, misleading smiles drawn in the blood of naughty little boys and girls who don't eat all their green vegetables. Tommy Logan down the street said that what they can't digest they give to the lions and tigers to dispose of. I can hear that kooky, squeaky clown car puttering down my street toward my house and wonder how many they stuffed into it as I pull the covers up over my head and concentrate on not wetting the bed, because Kyle Jacobs says the smell attracts and excites them. Can't sleep... clowns will eat me.

Rapture at the Santa Monica Pier

by Brian Steel

Maybe it was the woolen overcoat worn in the heat of July that spoke of miracles or the golden ski cap that resembled a halo. Maybe it was his ability to balance on a 24oz can of beer that recalled His walking on water. From between cracked and dry lips the words came slow at first, pushed out of his mouth and floating into the air on hungry wings; a new Sermon on the Mount for the 21st Century. But this is no longer the City of Angels; this is the end of America, the tip, the vanishing point, and his words are swept away by the mob of beach-bound unbelievers. When Jesus does return, he's going to need a better agent. I give him my card and from behind sunglasses say, "Call me, we'll do lunch."

Memories of My Sister

by Oceana Setaysha

Every time I walk into the kitchen the first thing I see is that photo of you as I sift through every memory, searching in vain for just one with you in it, while I lament at this cruel fate because I can't remember who you were, and I will never see who you might have become. The only time I ever see dad cry is when we visit your grave and even though I can't remember you I cry too but the only explanation I can think of is I am crying for never having known you like I wanted to. As I stare at your photo I find my subconscious thinking *what if?* and I know I could stay forever to contemplate what would have, could have and should have been. I didn't sleep for months before I turned 13 because I was so scared that, like you, I would fall victim to some silent killer and never live to be anybody more than that little girl smiling quietly from the photo in the kitchen, never aging, only fading on paper and in memories. But you will never fade in my memories because the only ones I have of you are imagined on long sleepless nights with clues from home videos and that photo in the kitchen. But some nights, I swear I can hear your voice echo in my dreams.

Red

by Rob Winters

The glass burst into the classroom, a powerful bullet leaves a perfectly round red hole in her head. People scream and take cover under desks like those old nuclear attack exercises during the cold war. Minutes go by, paranoia. The girl's hair is drowning in her blood. The sniper is never caught. You wake up years later, soaked in sweat.

We Woke Up One Morning

by Sophia Macris

We woke up one morning, Nick and Jeremy and I, when we were still getting enough sleep to get up early, and walked down to the beach. We swam for half an hour and then showered outside, and the air was still fresh and the sun was blindingly bright and I felt so good I resolved to stop drinking. As we walked back to the house we passed fields on the right, neatly planted rows of cucumbers and lettuces, melons and tomatoes. To the left was the house with the Trojan horse in the yard, which always reminded me of an abandoned set from a Fellini film. Nick lit a cigarette and I inhaled deeply, coughing from my post-swimming lungs, and he talked about Donne and I talked about Didion and I knew nothing, not my promise about alcohol, not the conversation, not the way the pavement felt on my bare feet, none of it would make a difference in the end. We said we'd start every morning with a swim but only did it once.

Bad Today, Good Tomorrow

by Madam Z

I have decided to re-write some of my life's stories, and give them happier endings than they had in the first telling; then I will repeat those new, improved stories to myself, over and over, until they, effectively, become true.   I'll start with my childhood: Mama didn't abandon my sisters and me when we were little; she stayed with Daddy and we had an idyllic childhood.   The plastic surgery on my harelip was a big success, and I looked "normal," and kids didn't make fun of me any more.   When I was sixteen and went for a walk with a neighbor boy and he lured me into the woods, where four of his friends were waiting, they didn't rape me, because I fought like a tigress and they ran away like frightened rabbits.   The bastards have horrible scars from the claw marks... *(god, this feels good!).*   Tomorrow I'll perform "plastic surgery" on some other ugly events and convert them to beautiful new "truths" and I'll keep operating until everything is perfect, and then maybe I'll write a book and tell everyone else how to reconstruct their lives, but first I have to fix that part of my life, where my foster mother told me I was just a worthless piece of shit and would never amount to anything, but she was wrong, goddamn it, 'cause tomorrow I'm going to be a famous author, and she can burn and rot in Hell.

The Origins of Chocolate

by Tim Horvath

Aidan spouted misinformation. To cite merely one instance from the innumerable that I have adduced over the years, he stated once at a party with absolute certainty that a canard was a type of animal, arboreal but prone to burrowing at higher altitudes, the only known species, he assured me, whose ears doubled as wings. It was not that he was ignorant - in fact, I've known few more learned - but rather that his parents had interlaced his childhood stories with such an epic cast of mythological characters, such congeries of marvelous event, that he was forever incapable of sorting out what was real from what was sheer magisterial invention. One night he walked me through the garden and, taking my hand aloft in his, pointed out "his" constellations: Gelemanda the Half-pomegranate, Agalarius the Peripatetic, Wadassa and her Daughters, Extractors and Synthesizers of Cocoa. That they lived in exile, victims of a bitter, endless war with our constellations, dodging Sagittarius's arrows and Capricorn's merciless hooves (even Libra's scales stung) brought him close to tears, yet I never saw him waver in his conviction that one day the cosmic array would be divvied up anew in some way agreeable to all.   I will always envy him his constellations.

Playing God

by Carolyn Carceo

It's not so easy, this playing God. You create a world, and then you decide who or what lives there - what people, what plants and/or animals, who's smart, who isn't, and who (if anyone) has special powers. Then, there is back-story - what events led to what's happening now. Who is your hero/protagonist - gender, species, commoner, nobility, flawed, perfect, young, old, in-between, alone, with a group, and does s/he succeed or fail? Now the fun part - telling yourself the story, and writing down what you hear yourself saying in your mind. All this so someone else learns the story of your world; only the Creator-of-all had ghostwriters - we lesser creators have to tell our own story.

Part 4

Refreshments

Two Friends, Six Hours, One Elevator

by Maggie Whitehead

Hour One: *Panic* - furiously press the emergency button, contemplate plunging to our deaths in this tiny metal coffin, embrace, share teary goodbyes, pace, cry, pray. **Hour Two**: *Outrage* - "This is ridiculous(!); how could this happen(?); such incompetence(!); such negligence(!); you better hope we die in here, because if we get out we're *so* suing your ass!!!" **Hour Three**: *Hunger* - sit, bemoan our grumbling bellies, calmly assess our resources, wisely decide to save the granola bar for later and split a tin of Altoids for now. **Hour Four**: *Betrayal* - "Hey, where's the granola bar(?!?); what do you mean you ate it(?); you bitch(!!!); well, guess what(?!); I'm sleeping with your husband(!); and I don't even *like* it(!!!)" **Hour Five**: *Apologies* - admit the whole husband thing was a lie born from jealousy and blind, maddening hunger; compare wounds; sheepishly return each other's clumps of hair and bit of fingernails; exchange compliments on fighting prowess, agility, and minty-fresh breath; stare awkwardly at the ceiling for a bit; move on to the neutral topic of whether or not the ceiling tiles are edible. **Hour Six**: *Release* - the metal maw of the elevator is finally pried open and forced to expel its prey: two friends - bloody, bruised, bellies full of peppermint and drywall - limp silently together towards first hospitals, then lawyers, then home.

Limbo

by Peter Holm-Jensen

When he's four, he'll need to go to nursery school. It'll be hard to let him go the first day. We'll spend Sundays at your parents', where he can play in the garden. When he's older we'll move to the countryside and get a dog. We'll get him lessons in whatever his talent turns out to be. But before we talk about the whens, we have to face the ifs, the ifs of incubation and respiratory failure, not to mention the whys.

Apocalypse Now

by John Parke Davis

I remember work was very empty that day. "Where is everyone?" I asked Bob Canady, as we poured thin, muddy coffee into our crappy Styrofoam mugs in the breakroom. "Rapture, don't you know," he said, shrugging his narrow shoulders. Counting the empty offices on the way back to my own, I was truly astonished to see how many of my workmates had been Good Christians - the criteria must have been considerably less demanding than I had previously been led to believe. On some level, I felt a little excluded. It passed quickly, though, and honestly, I was just happy that the self-righteous bastards were gone.

Not an Escape

by Saif Khan

I fell headfirst and kept falling — my cheeks never fluttered and my eyes stayed mostly moist. I thought about the days where one primitive man in striped fur roared at another for scavenging off his mammoth steaks — where the remainder of the pack thronged the two in tight circle; egging them to duel with howls and hisses and stones. The endless rock walls surrounding me repeated the same sharp edges and cracks and the dark abyss hovered unchanged beneath. I thought about my great-grandmother who had lived over a hundred years and who wore the same wedding band for eighty-five; and how an emaciated, unmasked gunman took it from her, breaking her finger while she laid in her last bed, in Karachi. I thought, *where am I going, and for whom?*, and as these images and questions blurred by I noticed something shiny approaching, a twinkle or glint in darkness; revved in anticipation I opened my pointed arms ready to take hold, but it passed too quick. I still plummet.

My Brother's Last Run for Swift

by Scott Beal

The sky's black mat flattens everything against the rush of road which undercuts him from the edge of his headlight beams. The cab seethes around him, panel and windshield buckling in with each gasp. The pavement's metronomic white dashes run him through — a seam, splitting. Five hundred miles away she sits his son in front of thawed nuggets and a cartoon sponge. Every minute at the wheel he rolls deeper into anesthetic panic, farther from nightlights and gladware. If he pulls off now for a mouthful of air, the cab will never let him back in.

Elicit This

by Diane Brady

Six beginner English language students, all adults, settle into their seats at the school, eagerly awaiting their introduction to a new group of ESL teacher candidates. A young man walks to the front of the class and begins the lesson; he speaks too quickly for the beginning students, but they are entertained by his flailing arms and body gyrations; even his fellow colleagues are unsure what he is doing, what word he is eliciting. After twenty minutes of blank stares, the young teacher checks his lesson plan and the clock; he steps behind the Chilean man and grabs him in a simulated choke hold; the Romanian woman shrieks; the young teacher smiles before moving to the Iranian and Palestinian men, seated side-by-side, and pokes a finger at each of their heads; the Indonesian woman gasps as the teacher approaches the Mexican man beside her and pretends to stab him in the chest. In the corner, the ESL teaching instructor, horrified, writes furiously on a copy of the young man's lesson plan; when the bell sounds, the young teacher, now frantic, sweat permeating his tailored shirt, picks up the marker, looks directly into the eyes of each language student and writes "T" on the whiteboard followed by eight lines. The instructor stands and announces there are two more candidates to present lessons; but the young man at the board ignores him and instead quickly fills in the missing letters – TERRORIST; he points to the language students and shouts – "You are all terrorists!" Simultaneously, everyone stands, language students scrambling, teacher candidates pushing the foreigners to move faster, ESL teaching instructor holding the classroom door open; the group safely exits the building as one gunshot fires inside.

Chorizo

by Peter Wild

There was something about chorizo she couldn't get enough of. Part of it was the flavour, the spice and the smoke in the meat, but it wasn't just the flavour; she dug the consistency of the chorizo too, how it felt both unchewed and hot on her tongue and then, greasy and giving, as she mashed it between her back teeth. It became something of an obsession, an obsession and a challenge, the challenge being to include chorizo in as many meals as she could. So, she took to slicing the sausage on her cornflakes in a morning, including the sausage between two slices of bread at lunch, cooking up the sausage with pasta at nights and even, when the craving proved more difficult to sate, plopped, floating, like a vein-y lily-pad, atop her creamy hot chocolate at the end of the day. Her husband did his best to understand but it was difficult, especially as the meat seemed to inflame his wife's passions, fanning and stoking her ardor even as his own libido cooled, something about the smell of spicy meat oozing from her pores getting in the way of his tumescence. He told her straight – "It's me or the meat!" – but (*too late!*) her mind was already made up.

191

Burnt Edge of Reasoning

by Elizabeth Feldman

Dreaming, please tell me I'm dreaming. I can't see, I can't see, my eyes, they feel like, okay, breathe I will try to breathe, but I feel as though I'm bound by some cloth with the smells of what seems like bubble-wrapped white fabric, faint but also ever so sinewy, and when the scent surfaces it scares me with the newness of this redolence whiff, such a vapor to it unknown and new, so new to me. I have to be dreaming, tell me please, because why can't I feel anything, or see anything, but feel painfully lighter, like I'm not supposed to be here, these intense sensations of time lapsed numbness feel as though they've embraced every part of me, but I still can't see and find the reason, and no one is coming to me, someone help me please, tell me why I can't see, please. No one is there, or am I just in this horrible dream with the constant sound of this beeping, and I don't know what it is, just beep beep beep all the time, as if it's following along with my heart, tempting my heart to pass up the beats of this mocking machine. Darkness, complete darkness, my skin and eyes, my entire body it seems is mummified, pressed up against this assaulting sweat-filled prosthetic and I just want someone to tell me if I'm dreaming, oh please someone, and I can't scream, my voice isn't there, it has to be a dream, someone tell me I am dreaming, please. She enters the room in white, giving off this floating glow to her, surrounding the room with the sounds of only her footsteps against the cold colorless room, filled only with sounds of the support machine that aids the body to move along with life even when the person cannot, and as she, the one dressed in white, approaches the declining life on the hospital bed, she reaches for the hand of her patient, the only part of her that wasn't affected by the inferno, and gently, she whispers to her, "rest, please, go to a good place and rest, go to where you won't hurt, go and dream, just dream and I will be here when we remove the bandages from your body."

The Key

by Tara Lazar

She recently gave him the key and today he entered the house without knocking, as if he has always lived here. I tried to ignore him by staying in my room, but he tapped on my door when she was out, knelt at my bedside, and asked me to smell his breath. I searched for Listerine but found none, handed over some crumbling Altoids from the bottom of my backpack, and mixed baking soda with lemon juice. When she returned home, they disappeared into her bedroom and the quiet meant she was happy. At dinner, he winked at me while passing a tureen of tuna casserole, as if we shared some magnificent secret. That's the moment he invited himself into my life, another place he did not belong.

What He Gave Her

by Monica Friedman

When they fell in love, she was five-one and weighed one hundred twenty-three pounds; he was five-eleven and three-fifty. After about three months, they moved in together and went halves on the grocery bill, except he ate about three quarters of the food. She felt cheated. She began to overeat to get her fair share, but she could never eat as much as he could. Six months later, she weighed one thirty-eight, and she had to leave him. She never even noticed that he'd lost fifteen pounds.

As Happy a Place

by Robert Prinsloo

Confused, I took out my heart, but then, not knowing what to do with it, I passed it on to the nearest person who I thought might. But she didn't seem to know either, so I took it back and looked around for someone better. When she came along she took it, tentatively listened to it, shook it a little, but then gave it back to me, so I tried the next person, who thanked me, but no-thanked me. Eventually a boy came along who did take my heart, though reluctantly at first, and then, walking off with it, just like that, next bin he came by, he trashed it. I watched it awhile then, pumping away at the bottom of the street-side waste bin on it's own. And in the end I left it there; it seemed as happy a place as any other.

Bruised Ego for Change

by A.R. Morgan

Change is easy when the ego is bruised. The hobbled limp of self-confidence is an uncomfortable reminder of what I don't want to happen again. That's what I tell myself this time. This is an opportunity for change. Of course, it works until the black-and-blued reminder fades away, leaving me healed. So, I do hope enough change happens before the ego gets better.

The Trouble with My Mind, Then

by Victor S. Smith

When the booze is pouring out of you, and you have the taste of an ashtray in your mouth, and you are lying down in a bed you don't recognize, with a woman you don't know, you have these moments where the world just makes sense. Then you have enough of them and you somehow manage to convince yourself that you have it all together; you show up to work, you meet up with your friends and everybody probably says you are going through a "rough time," but you know the truth. Or do you? Because that's the problem, you know. You tell yourself over and over again that you have it together, and you somehow start to buy your own bullshit. The lies become part of your history and you can't tell whether or not you actually did some of the stuff you claim: Gulf War vet, inventor of Excel, Black Belt in Mai Tai.

Sincerely Yours

by Bryce Carlson

Dearest Vegan, I am writing because there is a question which begs an answer from you: since you are of the vegan persuasion, and you refuse to eat anything that was once a living-breathing animal or any byproduct from such a being, is it against your personal religion to perform oral sex on your male counterpart? You have said that we, and by we I mean Homo sapiens, are simply evolved animals and that this serves as ammunition for your avoidance of said ingestion. Perhaps it is possible for you to get around the specific act of "chowing down" on a male phallus but then the question becomes this: is it against your personal religion to swallow a man's semen; can you even have it in your mouth? I mean, you would spit out a hunk of filet mignon if you found it in your organic salad – so how is a man's hunk of beef any different? Surely, consuming a human byproduct, such as ejaculate, would taint your pure body, proving you a hypocrite and a liar (oh, and I earnestly apologize to your male counterpart if this eliminates his reception of fellatio and said swallowing, which I'm sure he ever so much enjoyed). Sincerely Yours.

The Modern Love Letter

by Nicole Ross

I'm afraid that if you leave me, I'll forget which
muscle groups to strength train on which days. I
know that this sounds silly and trivial but you have
become my something silly and something trivial, my
everyday day to day. Sometimes when I'm running by
the water I look around and wonder: are there times
ahead when I will not miss crawling into bed and
resting my head on your outstretched arm? Then I
wonder other things, like whether or not I'd be
knowledgeable about energy-saving fluorescent light
bulbs without you, or whether I would have started
liking avocados as soon, and I try to figure out what's
more important to me than the everyday day to day of
us. In truth, this isn't what I thought it would be like,
because I used to believe (*maybe I still believe?*) that
love, real love, hits you like a gong, or like lightening,
or even like a steam roller and knocks you out with
its power and absurdity. But it doesn't, love is what
happens on the sidelines, in the whispered moments,
on the blurry edges of well-planned photographs.

Something to Say

by Jamie Boyt

We've come a long way since that night on the beach, when I killed that seagull. I didn't mean to kill it, I was just casually throwing rocks, wondering what I was going to do to get to the next level with you. I'd never have guessed that causing the death of a small bird would do the trick, or was it really the repeated hugging and nuzzling and begging forgiveness that did it? Either way, it worked and we bonded. But that night was just the beginning, and our love soon blossomed. Our two beautiful children are testament to that.

Slamming in a Flurry

by The Old Guy Up Front

There was a time when I would've thought, for sure, that he was running numbers, scrawling in a crouch on crumpled paper, shoulders curled for the cold Chicago wind and secrecy. He walked north on Columbus in one if those sifted December flurries. It could have been a profile video for the city's Facebook if it had one, you know, when tourists go gleeful and take pictures. He burrowed into the wind with scalp bald among cornrows, not glancing up, as do the young who know we're watching them be intent. I'd seen Saul's and Marshall's movies though, and knew the numbers he ran were rhymes and phonemes feeling real to him, and cold, barbarous in every way he could muster. Like him, I gamble daily, crunch syllables, look intently at the blank, wish my elders could know I know what they knew before they died, like him, a kid in flurry, making sentences and songs to slam against somebody's wall.

Forever Alone

by Christopher Kirk

She stood alone, forever alone, with headphones in her ears, leaning tiredly against the window, searching for true life in the alien wilderness beyond. There, the amorphous throngs of people recognized her gaze and ignored it. She knew no friends beyond those emotions and dreams that made her real. I approached, thinking I could console her, believing I could convince her that I, too, had emotions and dreams; that I, too, was not merely a personality, but a person, a being with flesh and tears and blood. But I stopped abruptly, for who among my own acquaintances meant more than another trivial conversation, more than another package of shared interests and behaviors, more than another wall my imprisoned soul could not hope to penetrate? Suffocated by doubts, I turned to the door and fled into the wilderness, leaving her and leaving me forever as we were - forever alone.

Passage

by Deborah O'Neal

In my home, I would keep white flowers all around, all the time. In that home, the doors and windows would stand open, welcoming the outside in. The breeze would blow through, quietly, wanting to caress the lovely white petals; gently, not wanting to alarm the newborn buds or disturb the peace and elegance of a drowsy head's last moments, not hasten the scattering of white, turned ivory turning brown, to the waiting welcoming table or floor. Gently would it carry the subtle, indefinable fragrance throughout the rooms and out the open portals, sharing with the green of summer, gold of autumn, the whiteness from inside. Delicately would it introduce the motion of each graceful, peaceful shade one to another, white to white, softness to grace, peace to tranquility. My house would be alive, would live and breathe a white fragrance, an inviting and welcoming peace, shared upon the air.

Husband Number Two

by Stephanie Wright

Husband Number Two – bless his heart – was the quasi-fulfillment of the need to be needed and the recognition of her own need for salvation. He showed up Saturdays and bought groceries, took the kid to the movies, and told her she was beautiful. The diamond he slid on her finger at twenty-six became a black leather collar enslaving her to his myriad addictions, and the hysterical laughter in her own head reminded her bondage was supposed to be fun. The second kid came at thirty, just in time to witness the master's degree and his first public meltdown. Four overdoses, one PhD, one dead father, and another baby later, and it was all over but signing the divorce papers. At thirty-seven, she figured it was a good thing indeed that adult novelties had improved considerably over the previous twelve years.

Luminous Specificity

by Tim Horvath

He's getting the best massage of his life, he thinks, the hands coaxing to life parts of his torso and even, if he can momentarily believe in such a thing, soul too, parts he's maybe lost, maybe misplaced, maybe misfiled by Janine as has happened so often lately, his secretary, once infallible, reliable as a parent in the eyes of a young child, then the holiday party, the incident, as they stood on the balcony and took in the overly-warm early December air, trying to raise eyebrows suggestively without coming off as bug-eyed, his exact words, "No mistletoe, and not like I can even do what I'd like to do next, you know," an utterance which had made perfect sense to him at the time but was far too oblique for the circumstances, after the number of drinks he'd consumed and she, he could sense, had consumed even more in sheer raw volumetric terms, not even factoring in differences in body weight and drinking history (his daily consumption of one or two, the cap of the Seagram's or Bailey's or Bombay or his favorite the thick, regal Hennessey like a second doorknob that ushered him fully into his apartment, like his whole living room was nothing but a giant foyer and he wasn't fully inside 'til he felt the liquid enter and become part of him, always capping the lid as he downed the first because that's what his dad used to do, a fragment of memory from his childhood lodged in him like a splinter, this ritual capping though it was obvious that a second and possibly a third would follow shortly, remembered thinking even then what's the point really, like some precious molecules might escape or some undesirable ones invade), his daily intake in contrast to Janine's, Janine who'd even said, "I just don't drink like this, I don't even, I don't even really drink," to which he'd responded "Tonight we're taking the lists of what we do and what we don't do and folding them into oriental cranes," which, even had he said what he had meant to, which was "origami cranes," would have been, though poetic and profound sounding, not the least bit original, was in fact virtually an exact reproduction of what something his son had said to him on the phone earlier that day from Chicago, though he actually lived in Jacksonville, what the fuck was his son doing living in Jacksonville, making him acknowledge the existence of Jacksonville, tying him to a long leash that ended in Jacksonville, forcing him to pay attention to weather patterns and hurricanes, one after the other like someone was churning them out, one-eyed freaks of nature, infants who should've been aborted but instead came shooting out by the dozens now, annually, a Baby Boom of hurricanes, he laughs to think of it, who'll support those hurricanes in their old age, who'll support *me* in my looming old age with all these needy hurricanes, hurricanes that have to go to school, hurricanes eating up tax dollars, he pictures the Caribbean suddenly as a giant classroom and all of the students unruly, throwing things erasers pencils flipping desks, now the maps lolling over the chalkboard flapping whipped around and the American flag jutting from the corner taken for a ride and her kneading of his flesh makes him long for more of this nonsexual physical connection if he could have this all the time he could stand being impotent, where is he though, oh yes, his son down in Florida, who might or might not be around in his old age, depends on so many things, he'd moved down there before the diagnosis to be closer to the hurricanes because an entrepreneur like himself had to, he'd told his dad, be closer to the source of them himself, had to walk the walk on top of talking the talk, if he was actually going to convince investors, would-be shareholders, NaturaSolve, Inc., with their motto he was so proud of they'd driven out twenty minutes onto Route 10 when he'd visited them down in Jacksonville just to lay eyes on the billboard he'd basically, not expecting the loan to be repaid anytime soon, paid for, "Natural Solutions to Natural Disasters," a motto that left him just shy of being able to extrapolate what the company did, couldn't drive into the heart of Your Business Model, the son being strangely tight-lipped about the actual operations, almost as if afraid that his dad was going to blab something up in New York and the competition would sink its claws into it at this critical early juncture, the crucial ingredient in some secret recipe for a company that would respond to (and solve) natural disaster crises via all-natural means, he pictures hurricanes pitted against one another, one knocking the other out to sea like Sumo wrestlers, sees viruses knocking each other out, too, why not considering how easily a virus can bring down the burliest wrestler? When he'd talked to his son earlier that day, the day of the holiday party, that is - couldn't just call it a "Christmas Party" anymore, had to pretend that they were all-inclusive thanks to the ethnic diversity in the company for which he'd been an outspoken proponent because he thought it the first step in upping business overseas, these things all start with personal connections, he'd thought at the time, hire a few people from India and some Malaysians, hire a bunch of Chinese because these are the folks who still have family back home, lotsa family along with direct access to them and their ears and wallets and pocketbooks, if they have pocketbooks, who cares if they use pocketbooks or squirrel everything away in holes in filthy shoes, money's money, right, and since our new hires will be traveling anyway to those countries, we don't even have to put them up in hotels, they've got plenty of places to stay, such was his rationale even though he never vocalized this reasoning at the meetings, made sure he came across not as some crass venture-capitalist materialistic imperialistic Pacman as his son would have called him while still in his pre-corporate, pre-diagnosis placenta, green but not yet willing to profit off it, but instead at those same meetings came off as a bonafide multiculturalist, a profoundly broadminded and ethically unassailable advocate of global thinking and local action - of course, in the end they'd gotten some invigorating, quirky hires out of this approach like Dae-Hyun and Balraj but the personal connections to distant markets that he'd envisioned never panned out since instead of going abroad and living cheaply and sending out tendrils

209

into the communities abroad what happened was that people vanished with company computers and Blackberries and secrets, went to Mumbai and never came back, any attempts to contact them via their families proving fruitless and then the strategy they'd meticulously mapped out in extra meetings and ordering in food and car service dropping everyone off at their front door at night suddenly materialized on its own in those markets, a company in Mumbai taking a similar approach producing comparable results mysteriously within six months of Balraj having been dispatched to India and while this had really only happened that once it seemed to him there was clear and present danger in having hired these different ethnics, because each of them now rather than being like a special operations liaison on the street in his/her native country able to speak the language of the natives and gain invaluable access to the backrooms and second floors and otherwise-skittishly-faceless IP addresses now became rather a liability, a spy for the enemy who might just export the secrets to precisely those already-shady and dubious characters lurking behind those tightly-clad doors and in those claustrophobia-inducing alleyways. "Fuck, that hurts!" he cried out; six vertebrae down, roughly, it was like she'd located and was currently working on popping a giant bunion underneath his skin. Was it any coincidence that his son himself had dropped out of college to take time to trot all over Southeast Asia, backpacking ostensibly, he thought, cringing that "backpack" was even a verb, that it was something you would "do" instead of something you'd carry, just as juvenile as "signage," which, even though he was as guilty as the next guy of using it, he

210

only did so because you had to speak in the terminology that was current, and so he'd make that concession, so there was his son wearing a backpack and spending the money that was supposed to have paid for a graduation trip to Austria to visit the side of the family that had remained and now instead he was traipsing around the Pacific Rim, probably getting rim-jobs too if his post-college experience - not really "post" because he hadn't graduated but he sure wasn't going back now, so yes, post-college experience was anything like what had gone on at Wesleyan, things he hadn't wanted his son to tell him about but which he seemed to be willing, even enthusiastic, to relate in all sorts of detail, such "luminous specificity" as the guy had put it in a class, Messinger was the guy's name, the class not in any school but at the Community Center, 20th Century Poetry, Valerie had pushed him into taking it so that they could find common interests, this was about six months before she left him maybe in part because he'd been so indifferent about the class, even resistant to being with the mostly sixtysomething and older crowd that was there to stave off Alzheimer's for a few years, that's what he said to her and three months later she'd divorced him in papers just full of luminous specificity about his misdeeds and slights against her, years-worth showing that she'd been keeping a running log including that line, each instance a brushstroke to paint him as cold callous vindictive petty brutish intimidating father husband with a sadistic streak, utterly self-absorbed, ironic that phrase "luminous specificity" since now there was all this stuff that he actually wanted his son to be correspondingly specific about, such as what exactly it was his company did, and whether they'd be interested in working together in targeting global markets, maybe even think about a merger of some sort, while there was still time to think about mergers and such, while he still could, but this was precisely when his son desisted from spilling all, although he did share the most circuitous personal revelations, such as the one that he'd told his father the morning of the Christmas, no Pan-Eurasian Holiday Party (don't leave out Australia and Antarctica, for crying out loud, he self-chastised, we'll get hit with a lawsuit from some penguin or research scientist from Under the Under), the revelation being that he'd met the person he wanted to marry should the law make room to accommodate such alliances and the way he knew this was that he'd been at the airport and he was sitting in front of his laptop and on came the screensaver which, quite simply it looked like the screen was a piece of paper that folded itself up bit by bit into a slight folded chunk of pixilated paper, smaller, in fact, then any actual physical piece of paper could be folded at least by human hands, some math teacher way back in the day had explained about the limit on the number of times a single piece could be folded, but this physically-impossible but visually-striking image of hyperenfolded paper had caught the eye of a youngish Japanese man who was sitting there all alone, and upon spotting it he'd stared at it and said, boldly perhaps, "Is it origami?" and of course his son, who knew not the first thing about origami, knew only how to check off the "Infinite Folds" box to generate this screen-saver on his computer, turned to him and said, "No, do you do origami?" and while unfortunately he didn't have

212

any folding paper - there is a special kind, he said, but he could make do with regular - and so his son had popped open his briefcase and pulled some company documents having to do with flood remediation and glanced at them as if to ask, "How badly do I need these documents for the meeting I'm about to go to in Chicago and do I need them more or less than I need folding paper in order to allow this lovely man to show me gently how to make miracles emerge and make me forget momentarily that I'm sitting at the brown-beige Nashville Airport?" And so he had taken one document and handed him another and, folding back one edge and running his nail along it then tearing to transform it into a square which was essentially turning it into something at least the shape and size if not the texture of actual Japanese folding paper, he began to guide him through making a swan, a lantern, a frog sitting on a lilypad followed by a stack of lilypads so he could make more on his own, and even after they'd exchanged phone numbers upon landing in O'Hare, his son not wanting to allow him to get away, even if it meant only that he would one day show him a few more origami constructions on a webcam, and even after he'd relocated from southern California to Jacksonville to be with his son, even six months later now that they live together and he has unlimited access to piles of origami paper he still takes business documents that were dedicated to the dousing of fires by natural means or whatever, he's guessing because he doesn't know what they actually do, but whatever it is he turns them into shapes, he's become famous for it, actually, had a lobby display for the company that turned into an exhibition and then starting offering a class for locals

213

called "Fold Your Frustrations," where they would take the documents that made them most distraught, memos that reprimanded or reiterated dress codes or made said codes more stringent and unreasonable especially for friggin' Florida; pink slips, speeding tickets, overdue credit card minimum payments at nonnegotiable 23.4% interest rates, rejection letters, "D" chemistry tests, divorce papers, adulterous correspondence turned up by significant others soon to be less significant and more other, printed emails or instant messages, insurance claims against, denials of benefits, positive test results, T-cell counts, FDA notices of trials and of the need for further trials, delay of FDA approval, even for experimental use, they'd take these documents and, two hours later they'd walk away with something beautiful and handmade, something that arched its wings or swiveled its head and, like sculpture manufactured from resuscitated garbage but much more personal managed to reclaim from the detritus of failure, the landfill of despair, shapes of magnificent triumph and unanticipated strength, and it was this which he must've been subconsciously mulling over when he'd made the remark to Janine six months ago that precipitated her swan-dive from her brilliant, almost unnervingly-efficient self, answering phones and word processing (a verb he could abide, barely) with precision and even elegance, pivoting like a skater and making him think that there ought to be an Olympics for secretaries and if there was one, she'd be eligible for at least the silver, a remark he'd thought about making but thought better of it for once, if only they knew the number of times he held his tongue and didn't make the inane, offensive, or

214

just awkwardising (there was a verb that needed to be, how else could you express it) comment, but it was always the one that you did make that hung in the air like flatulence at first but then went on to hound you for months, years, like the time he said to his son, "I don't care if you're queer or straight or whatever, just make up your mind so I know how to deal with you," and his son shot back, "Deal with me, Dad, is that what it's about?" and he'd rephrased it, said, "I mean approach you," and his son said, "Like what, like I'm holding people hostage, like I have a disease?" and he'd gotten more and more flustered and even when he'd gone off to Asia and done Lord-only-knows-what and found himself and figured it out, he didn't know how to approach his son, he'd said it before the news his son had HIV before his son knew it himself and so that knowledge couldn't have even been down in the bowels of his mind even though the thought had crossed his mind more than once but still, after the fact the line had stuck out there like the howls of that guy who was a front-running candidate for President until the news media had played his wolf-like yelping ad nauseum and maybe that was the thing they would remember most about him, poor sap, though he was glad at the time to see the guy out of the race because what did he have to offer him; even before the media, though, before television and the Internet and any of it we had the memories of those around us which would trap our statements, capture us at our worst and play it back over the course of a lifetime, edited just as effectively and mercilessly and even vindictively as sound-clips are nowadays, and that's what seems to have happened with Janine, too, because he senses that everything is different, that the sense of trust that

215

he has always had in her as a worker and as a person is no longer reciprocated, his very gaze a leer to her and the simplest request a proposition, that this is bearing on her job performance, but he cannot reprimand her for it because she will call him on it, will quote him back to all of them, and it will not be the first time that these allegations were made, as before Janine there was Sharon and while that was consensual and even on her initiative, it has taken him two years to shake its memory and build up enough client synergy and promotional incentive clout that it's finally not the first thing they think of when they see him in the elevator in the hallway in the morning. Now he feels hands benignly karate-chop from his lower back to his upper and he's suddenly overjoyed that he asked for twenty minutes instead of his first impulse of ten because this has been one astonishing massage, one he really needed, and for a moment he thinks it might even pay to stretch this out to a half hour and plunk down an extra few bucks but he won't because he does have a flight to catch and should check voicemail and anyway, it occurs to him it might be good to scribble some of this down on a scrap of paper now while it is with him in all of its, ah – "luminous specificity" – sometimes the mind clings to okay things, too, he thinks, redeeming things like these words of Messinger, even if he thinks Messinger (unintentionally) sounded the death knell in his marriage because when Val saw him up there waxing eloquent about Stevens and Bishop she must've seen exactly what she was missing and must've seen, too, that they were never going to turn into one of those sexagenarian couples that would go off and take

216

classes together in "Buddhist Flower-Arrangement" or "The Florence that Dante Knew," still Messinger's words at least he'll always have or will, at least, until he doesn't, till he can't (ironically enough) stave off Alzheimer's or whatever it is that comes to get him, comes to steal everything the least bit luminous and specific and leave behind something (not even someone) dark, hazy, general, and he knows that to be nothing specific and to "be" only in general is to be lost, whether in business or in personal matters, knows he needs to fight against that as long as he can, even aware that insofar as he is fighting it he is only exactly like everyone else, and consequently in some odd sense the fight is already lost, over like this massage, as she lifts her hands while he continues to lie there and now hears what must be her running her hands under water and saying, gently, "Take your time," which he planned to do anyway, only when he feels ready lifting his head just slightly, next propping himself onto his elbows, then turning on his side, bending and extending each leg several times, and only then arriving on his feet, alive or at least remarkably life-like, unfolding parts of himself one at a time, eager to find out what she's turned him into.

The Unraveling of Mr. Pimm

by Joseph Grant

This is the story of Mr. Pimm, Gordon Pimm to be exact, don't ever call him Gordy, as he would not like that, no, no, no, it is the more prim and proper first name of Gordon that his parents bestowed, perhaps foisted upon him is the correct term, but nonetheless the only name he ever answered to was Gordon. At work, he was first-rate, a first-rate ass kisser, mirroring his career on that of his bosses, but it never got him anywhere because all of the executives were cut from the same handsome, athletic, six foot-two fine Ivy League cloth and with his own hair seceding away from the warty wasteland that was his scalp, only an island of thin wisps remained floating over the balding sea of his forehead, tsk, tsk, what a ridiculous-looking man in his cheap, off-the-rack suit, never to rise past a certain, already pre-determined corporate plane. Each day and every day, rain or shine, Mr. Pimm would board the 7 o'clock bus to catch the 8 o'clock train to get to his 9 to 5 job, always carrying his briefcase and his newspaper, which he folded underneath his arm, and he would daydream about getting a cheap, economical car, but in his gray-to-gray existence, he always kept this contemplation just beyond reach. Anal to a fault, he kept his personal relationships even farther and his concerned and busybody coworkers tried in vain to set him up with their obese cousin or their old maid sister, but each time, Mr. Pimm was, as his report card once read: "Virtually useless in social situations due to high level of non-personality." Alas for Mr. Pimm, he was neither interested in love or children, whom he thought of having once just as a tax dodge, but the pitter patter of little write-offs had to wait as his company merged with another, his department was outsourced and the soulless corporate Ken dolls that ran his company, ran it into the ground, his career mirror shattered, the reflection of whom he aspired to be in a thousand pieces on the ground. Until one day, Gordon Pimm was so tightly wound, he just began to unravel, for without love, without purpose and without humility, something popped within him and the human earth that made up Mr. Pimm unraveled in dusty spools into the thin air, floating... floating... floating and finally dissipating on the wind until there was no more Mr. Pimm.

Subdivision

by *Teresa Tumminello Brader*

They awoke to towering walls, much too high to see over, surrounding the camp they'd been corralled in yesterday. After Norman went to the entrance of the compound to help some new arrivals, Althea saw rows of elderly people shuffling toward her. She understood that they were the first wave of those to be eliminated, their fate being the eventual lot of the whole community. Althea felt an irrational need to return immediately to what she and Norman called home now, a straw hut with a dirt floor containing nothing but a cook stove. She darted through the compliant shambling procession and remembered the quarter of a chicken she'd cooked earlier that day, meat and bones simmering in a small saucepan of spaghetti gravy. It was all they had.

Time Travel

by Shaindel Beers

She spent large snatches of time wondering about
various people from her past — where they were, what
they were doing, if they were even still alive, if they
ever spent time wondering about her. Case in point
— the child prodigies she had tutored years ago
(because they were the only children she had ever
really liked, and she was chosen to tutor them
because they were second and third graders who read
at college-level, so naturally, their elementary school
teachers didn't like them, and their parents wanted
them to feel what it like was to be challenged by a
teacher). Also, the students at the inner-city middle
school where she taught; she didn't want to believe
they would be in their twenties now, and she had a
sinking feeling in her gut every time she heard
statistics about "at-risk" youth and wished she had left
her contact information for them at the end of the
school year. Then, there was the man on the bus one
commute home; something about standing together,
holding on to the aluminum bar was one of the most
intimate moments of her life — it was like spooning
standing up. There had been a baby asleep on his
mother's shoulder, and she had smiled at the baby,

and the man had smiled at her, and when she got off at her regular stop and had walked most of the way home, she heard running behind her, and she turned around, and the man held a note out to her and said, "Here's my number," and she had stammered, "I'm m-m-married," and he stuffed the note back in his pocket, sunk his shoulders into himself and walked away. He was a black man with cappuccino colored skin and mocha freckles scattered across his cheeks, and soft green eyes, hidden behind glasses, and she was afraid he would think it was "a race thing," because she was white and blonde, and her eyes weren't even blue, they were grey — never had she felt so devoid of color — so she pointed to her ring so he'd know that it was true, but it wasn't anymore, and some days, she still wondered where he was.

So Far Ecology

by Rachel Green

It's been a while since I vacuumed behind the sofa; a good few weeks at least, perhaps even a month or three. I dared to look underneath it today, pressed my face against a carpet that used to be what the shop referred to as "fist snow" but after three years looks more like "roadside sludge" and peered beneath the faux-velour fringe that edges the suite like a picket fence. It wasn't pretty. I'm quite certain that the dust bunnies have evolved into a semi-sentient life form because I could see evidence of primitive farming and a hunting party of dog-hair balls were attacking an old chocolate wrapper. I was left with the housewife's eternal dilemma of having a clean house or allowing a new species to evolve. Unwilling to make the decision I moved house, leaving the ecology of number 23 to fend for itself.

On College Applications

by E.Y. Kwee

They suck the life out of me — I'm trying to be successful, trying to lay the base for a good life, trying to set my destiny on track and I'm only 17. They. Want. Me. To do. *Everything!*

Self - Contained

by Rebecca Pigeon

Even at rest he is active, with a twitch at the ankle, at the end of a long leg. Arms wrapped around his midsection look still, but there is kinetic tension there. Such a lithe and elegant system, you might think he is ready to start out at any second, but he is actually at ease. The constant drumming of fingers and lifting of shoulders makes him appear high strung and reactive but he is neither. Every decision he makes is purposeful and well thought out with hardly ever a misstep or gaffe. I wonder if his ceaseless movement is some kind of impulse control and that if I secretly drugged him, the resulting muddled dream of his life would look more like a drunken carnival than a well-ordered closet.

The Invitation

by Melody Gray

Her road was long. She climbed into the car that pulled up beside her, it felt familiar, he felt familiar and comfortable like a recurring dream; maybe it *was* a dream. She leaned back in the seat next to him, adjusting her headphones; she heard the same song humming in her ears that was playing on his radio. She saw his arm was raised slightly and arched, his invitation for her to take hold. Slipping her hand through, she felt a sense of calm; her body liquefied further into the seat. "I'm tired," she said, sinking deeper, falling asleep in the stranger's car, drifting peacefully as he listened to her breath.

Blue Ice

by Diane Brady

The sounds are haunting – cracking snow bridge, icy wind roaring across the glacier surface, creaking rope, your voice calling to me from below. I imagine the horror I cannot see, bloodied face, shattered arm, dangling upside-down, staring at curving blue ice as it disappears, your weight pulling me closer and closer to the crevasse lip. Cold, oh so cold, my body shivers. With great effort I kick the front points of my crampons deeper and lean my upper body over the ice ax. Hours pass; exhausted, the silence between us deafening. When I cannot hold on any longer, I shout your name but you do not answer, so I reach for the knife, my teeth around the edge to open it, shaking, crying, praying for forgiveness while I sever the rope that links us.

Young Love

by Philip Alexander Rex Velez

Because of you I feel alive, because of me I can't deny. Once upon a time, not long ago, I fell in love with a girl. It was you, yes, it was you. And I'm wishing right now that you would see how you saved the life of a man in dire need. It was me, yes, it was me. And I take a deep breath and sigh, and I see you inside my mind.

A Very Civil War

by Robert Clay

We gathered up beneath a giant black summer storm cloud with lightning flickering far above. To our left we could hear the nervous snorts of Cromwell's cavalry. I think they were unsettled by the storm, or the impending battle, or maybe they just didn't like being so close to the nightmarish forest of our 18 foot infantry pikes that pierced the sky. I looked to the distant ridge where the King's army was hastily forming ranks, for we were offering battle unusually late in the day. I thought of my older brother, who years ago would take me fishing, hunting and riding through forests and green fields of a land not yet torn by war. He stood somewhere on that ridge, fighting for the enemy and I might see him before this day was out, I might even kill him.

Memory

by Maura Campbell

Bread may be the staff of life but memories are the stuff of life. Life stripped of memory is a life without personality. For what are we without the personal memories and moments that make up our being and bind our collective hours of existence together? Without memory there is no me. I, you, we become hollow shells of the selves we were. So, if I must choose, give me cancer or heart disease or a mild stroke perhaps but please leave my memories in, with, of, and to me.

When Tulsa Comes to Chicago

by Brian Steel

"Tulsa" was back. That's what she called him anyways, because he always wore that blue trucker hat with the big, red, block letters that spelled out the city where he was from. She always made up nicknames for the men she slept with in her life, a habit she had formed in high school with Jimmy "False Start" Drabinski; and so the man in front of her with the trucker hat, with the wide shoulders and the big, gentle hands that held a fresh cup of coffee she had just finished pouring for him, could only be called, "Tulsa." "How's my favorite Windy City girl?" he asked. "Just fine, until you showed up," she smiled, playing with the zipper on the front of her lime-green uniform. And after he had ordered, when he passed her back the menu, she brushed her fingers against the back of his hand and he smiled, as the steam from his coffee curled in ribbons above his shoulder; like a highway she ached to be on.

Late Nights at Bruin Café

by Samuel Sukaton

I feel like a real college man when I make a B-Caf run
late at night. There's a sense of self-forgetfulness in
burying myself in talking with friends with a tea latte
or a cup of black coffee until the wee hours of the
night that's just addicting, especially when I can sleep
in the next day... but even when I should just go off
to bed. Part of me came to college just for that - the
ability to play with the great stories and questions
of the human condition with friends, peers, equals,
without a care in the world, not even caring about
each other's baggage - one's gay, the other's a
Communist, another's a compulsive masturbator (just
as an example, not that any of my friends have any of
this baggage in spirit and truth). The lights of one of
the great cities of the world glow off in the distance, a
breeze moves the palms to that sleepy subtropical beat
that the Southland's so famous for, and the
conversation moves, freewheeling like the stars in the
sky - or the ones in Hollywood, for that matter -
blowing gently like the California breeze, as truth flies
in the wind, under that deep velvet night, and
tongues run loose. My voice dances on, but my eyes
slide to the crop of Bruin women, in jackets, or

pajamas, or just the typical jeans and shirt, and I smile at my weakness, knowing that another part of me came for just that: the atavism of togetherness in the night, damning the darkness, examining truth and beauty through sight and sound, crowding the air, caring for nothing more than the quality of company we are with, which is far beyond what we deserve. But, whether it's my mind or heart that moves me... I really love late nights at B-Caf.

My Defense

by Sara Crowley

She fell from the second floor window that she was cleaning. She fell from the window that she was cleaning because the window cleaner had struck her off his list. She fell from the window that she was cleaning because the window cleaner struck her from his list after she argued with him when he told her she still owed him for the last time. She fell from the window that she was cleaning because the window cleaner struck her from his list when she argued with him when he told her for the umpteenth time that she still owed him money. She knew that she damn well did not and that he was just a greasy scammer. I stabbed the window cleaner because my wife fell from the window she was cleaning as a result of our ex-window cleaner's attempt to scam her which resulted in her paralysis.

Goodbye Uncle Jake

by Alun Williams

When I was fifteen, my dad drove me down to St Louis. We were going to attend my Uncle Jake's funeral. Uncle Jake had a jazz band leading his coffin that sat on a carriage pulled by two black horses. People cried and sang and laughed. Uncle Jake must've been a helluva guy. I hope my funeral will be like that.

Out of Breath

by Nathan Tyree

I am out of breath. That's not to say that I was breathless; I don't think that quite conveys what I'm trying to say at all. It seems that there is a fine difference in meaning between those two phrases; a certain implication of the first that is missed entirely by the second. To be breathless seems to suggest, to connote (if you will) that you are panting, gasping to get more oxygen. To be out of breath, on the other hand, seems to suggest that you have no more breath left; there is something terminal in that construction. I am not breathless; I am out of breath.

Annual Art

by Louise Yeiser

"I've never seen this art exhibit before," I said. "I know it's here every year, but I've never stopped in to see it." When Jay asked me *why not*, I tried very hard to meet his gaze, rather than stare at the Burberry plaid print that I hated so much, that everybody wore, and that shouted and flashed at me from behind his crisp, navy blue Brooks Brothers jacket, and answered, "Because I'm white – not only white, but blonde – and I figured I wouldn't get it." "What's to get?" he asked. Trying not to feel annoyed, I turned my full attention to his face, with its slight touch of a summer tan from about two weeks before, maybe three, before feeling my eyes glide past him, to a tall, African-American woman, draped in flowing, green gauze, with a matching fabric braided through her hair, who was gesturing with her long, slender arms, and pointing and laughing, while she explained something to a small crowd that was gathered around her; and I could hear her voice's lilt, which reminded me of bob whites in the morning. "Exactly," I said.

Diet 100: The "T" Plan

by Jennifer Moore

Okay, so I've tried countless diets and slimming gimmicks over the years, but this time it's different – this time it's going to work. I can feel it. Here he goes, Fred the tapeworm, slipping down my throat easy as anything. Of course he's only little right now but he's got great potential. You feeling hungry yet, Fred? What'll it be then, cake or chocolate?

Love

by Rob Winters

The volition to live is gone, the spark has vanished and he feels empty. He feels like his soul has given up on his flesh, left before the last ray of light is lost in the void behind his eyes. "No," is what she said, and it hit him with a shockwave of depression. The rest of his days have been a farce, a selfless act to inflict no needless misery on those close to him. He is drained of everything now, reason never stood a chance. Love killed him with the simple inevitability of a single whispered word, with death inflicting efficiency.

Theory of Mind

by Jason Davis

"I don't love you," she said, "not anymore, I think," and that made good sense to me. She'd been two-stepping around me for months now, hesitant feet on the carpet, quickly shutting laptop screens and cell phones, and she only smiled when she thought I wasn't looking. I'd become a brick mason, putting up invisible sheetrock; white walls of white noise and structural framing going up in our shared un-shared house, to bear the added load. We were careful not to bump accidentally in the night, treading not too near one another, palms up and facing inwards, a discrete distance apart as we spiraled counterclockwise versus clockwise, outward and away. I knew, and she knew that I knew, but neither of us let ourselves know it. Speaking it, her voice hushed and sad, and worn clear out, I think that at last, at least, we're agreeing again.

My Father's Radio Career

by Christen Buckler

He recorded one advertisement, only one. It played for years, even after he died, even after we moved away and forgot how to mourn. My grandmother called me on some normal Tuesday; she was shelling peas for dinner. In the background, the gospel music she was listening to (loudly, so my grandfather could hear it as he read the paper in the living room) switched suddenly to a commercial break. *Come on down to Smith Chevrolet, we'll treat you like family - at Smith Chevrolet, everyone knows how to have a good ol' time.* I'm suddenly sitting on my cold tile floor and my grandmother whispers *honey, honey, darlin', I'm so sorry* and he still talks in the background like he's standing in that kitchen, like he didn't leave his baby behind.

Prognostication

by Doug Wacker

It will be black and will smell like burning, like a stalk of a sweetgrass placed over the hot coals of a supper fire. It will start as a ball of fiery glory tumbling through the dark nothingness of the Big Empty, and end no more than a malformed orb of compacted dust and a few pocked-marked pebbles. It will come to rest in the center of our sacred lake, near the island where the spiraling temple of our fertility god, Anshonie, was built by our fathers' fathers. The orb will sit undisturbed for many moon cycles, adrift in cool deep waters, until the warm harvest sun melts the snows on the westward slopes, causing the banks of the rivers that feed the lake to rise, leading to a tumult that will push the orb towards the sun-bathed banks of that rocky island. Inside one of the pockmarks on the orb will rest a little mass of cosmic ice. Within that ball of frozen gas will awaken a minutely infinitesimal pinpoint smattering of organic matter that will radically change our world, killing every sentient being, and, thus, paving the way for a new era, with new rulers, which will be known as the Era of Man.

Buffet Pirates

by Miz Yin

After the long drive to Seattle, we finally arrive at the hotel; we lug the many heavy bags up to the elevator, up to the third floor, to our rooms; the kids in one room, parents in another. We settle in; the television is turned on; I hook up my laptop and wait while it loads. While my sister pours her gripes with the parents into her Myspace blog, my brother eats chips on the bed, watching Cartoon Network and laughing with his mouth full of crumbs; they spill out as he gasps for air after the man is hit with the frying pan. Meanwhile, my father knocks on the door; I quickly answer it, and he brandishes the "Club Level" card; we head out toward the exclusive club lounge; our jackets picked specifically for the numerous pockets. We enter the room and head straight for the buffet tables, our greedy fingers itching to load up as much food as our arms and pockets can carry; we grab whole pieces of cake, bags of chips, ice cold soda pop, cheeses, delicious fruit, Chinese dumplings, and anything else that looks appetizing. We head back to our respective rooms; our roommates singing our praises; because to them, we are the beloved Buffet Pirates.

Pharming

by Linda Simoni-Wastila

The small room reeks; yellow urine puddles by the john, streamers of toilet paper and clods of crap circle slowly in the bowl. I do my thing, then cling to the sink as white and grey dots skitter across my open eyes. A hot, heavy fullness bubbles up my throat; an urge to vomit up all the chemicals strikes but I swallow it down, blast the faucet and splash myself with water. Bloodshot eyes stare back from the glittering glass, the green of iris obscured by vacant, opaque cisterns. I shake my head, but nothing changes; the stranger gazes back at me. Someone bangs on the door, so I turn from the sink, stagger to the ballroom.

Hiding My Face

by Tommy Hall

I have worked very hard to hide my face from the world (meaning everyone I love). Through smiles and fake laughter I cover who I really am and because of this I have become less of a man. Once I believed I could have changed everything about myself and just lived the life that everyone wanted me to have (not as easy as the preacher made it sound), yet I discovered that it could not be done. So I am going to just sit here and wait for the answer to come, because when you search and fight, that is when everything falls apart. If you want you can join me, but I will warn you, I won't really let you in. Even after I call you my best friend, you still won't know me.

Losing It

by Arris Leighton

The weight-loss surgery was successful and soon, over a hundred pounds melted away. My jutting bones are the headstones where my rolls and dimples used to live. My fat friends see me as the mirror that reflects their perceived flaws and have banished themselves from what they consider my judging eyes. My fat vanished, as did my husband, closely followed by our marriage. All that was left was the real me. When people ask how much I've lost, I reply, "Everything."

Part 5

Descent

The Next Bestseller

by Peggy McFarland

I write. I backspace. I think. I drum my fingers on the keys - alksjdfhakjdhkajdhf. "I suck!" I yell. The End.

Home?

by Jason Davis

All the lost people came back yesterday. No one can remember how long they've been gone and it's uncomfortable wedging them back into our lives, like putting on old boots, and you're wondering whether they shrunk or your feet somehow mysteriously grew. All of the spare bedrooms are offices now, and no one really wants to move their stationary bikes and printers. The returned wander aimlessly around our houses, opening refrigerators, pouring without interest over our CD racks, and thumbing through creaking faux-leather photo albums. They're as uncomfortable as we are. No ones knows what to say, and we all avoid eye contact, all of us wishing that all of them would just evaporate again so we could still pretend that we wanted them back.

Tornado

by Monica Friedman

I never saw it. The sky turned green and the clouds hung low over campus, but the only noises seemed far away. Distant winds. Joe herded us all into the basement of the library when the weather radio gave the warning. The power went out and we had only quavering fluorescent emergency lights for the two hours he held us captive down there. Student workers, professors, townies, we were all trapped together, but we could hear Joe running around on the main floor like a pirate captain navigating his ship through a storm.

Euphoria

by Jamie Boyt

I am filled with a sense of total bliss, more than ever
before. I can't help but turn my face toward the sky
and shut my eyes. My lips are pursed, as if in an
exaggerated kiss, and a low moaning noise escapes
me. If anyone were to walk in now, I'm sure they'd
laugh, or more likely, scream and run. The image of
me gurning, naked as the day I was born, is surely too
much for anyone. Even so, I will definitely be having
chocolate cake for breakfast again tomorrow.

Afraid of the Dark

by Juliana Perry

My earliest memories of my dad are oddly of his private practice office. I recall being placed in a dark and empty exam room with a Beta video player and a cartoon-style patient movie about Scabies, a parasite, more vivid in my childhood memory than Bugs Bunny. I was about 6 years old, too imaginative for my own good, and very impressionable. The images of bulging pregnant momma Scabies with grappling hooks, climbing the heights of human shoulders, passing moles the size of houses and forests of hair follicles, only to pull out a shovel, dig a nice warm hole in the subcutaneous layer of skin and erupt with hundreds of baby Scabies will forever be burned in my memory. Looking back at my childhood, it makes certain experiences clearer in retrospect. I understand why as an adult I am still afraid of the dark.

Inductive Reasoning

by E.Y. Kwee

When you're around, my heart skips spaces like the gaps in an 80-year-old man's dental work who has never once brushed his teeth. It aches like the delicate taste of snowflakes on a sugar-starved tongue. It pounds like a hippopotamus thumping across dry African sands and wild grass. It melts like pungent vanilla ice cream in a thick puddle under the scorching gaze of the early afternoon sun. It thrusts with the alacrity of vomit hurling out of my throat. So this is love.

The Spark

by Tara Lazar

The smoke alarms go off at 2:43am, their piercing shrills disconnecting your dreams. Smelling no smoke, you consider it a fluke, until you hear his voice calling from the guest room, "Get up! Get up! Get out!" You rifle through the bedside drawer and grab the wedding photo, wrap a sheet to cover you, and meet him in the hallway to dash down the stairs and out the front door. Outside you both examine the house, the windows, the bushes for signs of fire, smoke, smolder, but there's nothing. He's cradling a pillow, thinking he had saved the cat, so you both ease into laughter and decide it must have been fumes from the furnace, kicked on in a rare September frost. He holds the door open and, with your finger tracing the curve of his arm, you invite him to your bed — *won't you please come hold me and keep me safe, like you used to?*

Injury Prone

by Maggie Whitehead

I was nine years old the first time it happened. Drunk
on comic books and still unschooled in basic physics,
I jumped – as elegantly as my obstinate awkwardness
allowed – off the roof of our ranch house, fueled
by visions of Superman and neighborhood glory;
visions that shattered as quickly as my collarbone.
You arrived first, held me while mom's hysteria
rendered her impotent, whispered that everything
would be alright, that you'd make sure of it, and that
you loved me - all things I'd heard you tell my sisters,
but never once before told me. Of course it hurt, but
the pain was quickly muted by something else – *joy*.
For fifteen minutes – the time it took for the
ambulance to arrive – it no longer mattered that I
preferred comic books to football, that I was better at
writing than making friends, that I was quiet and
spindly and nearsighted and was probably doomed to
always be so, that – despite sharing your DNA - it was
an incredible stretch for anyone to believe that I was
actually your son. Since then it's been nine years,
three broken bones, forty-seven stitches, two 1st
degree burns, seven sprains, and myriad scrapes and
bruises, each born from the vain hope that I might

recreate that one moment – the *best* moment – the one when you told me you loved me; as if hearing a thing said is enough to make it true.

Infected

by Rob Winters

I can see them behind my veil sometimes, when the gray layers are touched by the soft stroke of the wind. They are all happy, appearance or not, and every smile or friendly gesture feels like a relic from forgotten times. I've read the Bible many times and I remember the second chance, the second chance even the worst of sinners got, but not me. Mad hysteria would follow this train wreck of thought on numerous occasions, but it does not anymore. It does not make the slightest difference when there is no remedy and God is but a fragment of our imagination. My life consists of one truth, and one truth alone, it is gone, put beyond the reach of redemption.

Husband Number Three

by Stephanie Wright

Husband Number One and Husband Number Two – bless their hearts – did their jobs well. Fool her once, shame on him; fool her twice, shame on her. There would be no Husband Number Three. As maturity, motherhood, and obligation set easily on her shoulders, she began to wonder what all the fuss was about, and she began to muse... crafting Husband Number Three from idyllic fancy and the cumulus dreams punctuating a sultry summer. The image grew to monolithic proportions, and as he came for her, his feet left prints in the ground larger than any mortal could hope to fill. She reckoned the dreams wouldn't keep her warm in her old age, but they'd cost her a hell of a lot less than the pound of flesh memory demanded.

Goodbye

by Li-Ann Wong

How do you say goodbye to someone you haven't seen in awhile and are not really close to but feel a close affinity with? I haven't seen you in a year, and now, I will never see you again - except in shades of sepia within yellowed crinkled pages where your easy smile and once-chubby cheeks will reside always. But of course it will never be enough, because I can never hug you again. Bringing myself to peer over the brink - your former fullness now reduced to a skeletal frame barely filling a 3 x 1, your familiar yet alien face - was the hardest thing in the world to do. How do I say goodbye when they close your face to the world forever? How do I say goodbye when I watch what's left of you consumed by hungry flames, wafting into the smoky heavens?

Old Friends

by caccy46

It's always bittersweet when it's time for me to put my dear friend to sleep, carefully trimming her down while we whisper lovely thoughts to one another of the past season, share new ideas about possible changes, make complaints about crowding, needing more sun, water or space and sharing thanks for the ways we demonstrate our love. I rake all the fallen leaves and create a blanket to help her keep warm during the long, snowy winter and pat them down as one would cover a baby with her crib blanket. She softly says "Thank you for your kindness, for you always make sure my needs are met." "Ah no," I reply, "it is I who should thank you, old friend, for each spring you excite me with your sudden return - brilliant, green sprouts shouting their contrast to the blanket of leaves is a truly exciting time of year for me - this year was your most beautiful one yet - your show of strength, abundance - growing so close to each other you needed dividing and new babies sprouting in surprising, distant places. It is you who delights me and all who pass by with your textures, shapes, colors, aromas and blooms. Spending hours with you is an intimate reconnection, learning more about how to make you feel and look your best - this is just one of your gifts to me. Let's not argue about who gives each other the greatest pleasure - we are old friends who will care for each other until the end."

Discipline

by Monica McFawn

The headmaster sat us down, made us link our hands
behind our chairs and wait so we would better dread
what was to come. He walked up and down the rows,
flipped a textbook's pages in each of our faces,
stopped at a dumb kid's head and pressed the book to
it, shutting his eyes as if willing the knowledge to
transfer to the student's brain. He pressed and
pressed and pressed and sweat came out on his
forehead and all the while the student just grunted
and bore it, and the rest of us became more and more
anxious, anticipating one or the other breaking down.
It was supremely uncomfortable, watching the scene
between the two of them, not knowing if we should
intervene, not sure if that would be breaking some
rule, not knowing what the kid's grunt meant or why
the headmaster kept squeezing his eyes shut harder
and harder, like he was bearing down to birth the
whole scene. It went on so long we imagined how the
book must feel pressed there, how the kid's neck must
be getting kinked holding up against it, how the
headmaster's shoulders probably hurt, how veins in
his eyes were likely popping, how both their minds
were probably wandering, thinking of scenes of their

respective childhoods, thinking of hot chocolate or other comfort things, or how they might have moved beyond thought into totally embodying their respective actions: grunt and press. As disturbed as we were, we began to fear the awkwardness and inadequacy of trying to address what was happening once they stopped so we could no longer even wish for it to end and then it occurred to us: this was the punishment.

In the Fog

by L.R. Cooper

Oh my God... I *hate* this feeling, I am so tired of living my life like this! The fog is so thick today it feels like it's grabbing my legs, trying to drag me down. *What was that* - I hear noises... could there be others like me out there somewhere? They don't seem to be scared or upset or anything, just noisy. Was that a laugh; is there a dog barking? As long as I can remember I have felt like I was on the outside looking in through a fog, always through a fog... this is no way to live.

First Love

by Steve Talbert

Infatuation. Hesitation. Trepidation. Acceptance. Connection. Elation.

Broken Beads

by Peter Wild

Okay so I want to tell you about Jan - this is a story
about Jan you could say - but Jan comes with baggage,
kind of, because, you know, I can't talk about Jan
without talking about New York and if I'm talking
about New York then you have to know that it's New
York in 1968 that I'm talking about and when I say
New York I don't want you getting hung up on which
New York I'm talking about (because, hey, *your* New
York might be different from *my* New York, right
man?) so let's be clear about all of this up front: I'm
talking about the Lower East Side, generally, and
Tompkins Square Park specifically and like I say it's
1968 sort of September October time. I'd been living
in Tigard, Oregon with my folks and I'd been seeing a
girl there by the name of Jodie and Jodie was great,
everything I wanted from life at the time, so I
thought, but then Jodie got bored for whatever
reason and ditched me for some stupid jock asshole
and I was all broken up and so my folks packed me
off to my sister in the city, thinking if anyone could
sort me out it would be Kitty. Kitty, you should
know, was shacked up with her girlfriend Amy and
Amy's kid Glory - Glory being short for Gloria, not

that anyone ever called her Gloria although for a little while there I got away with Glo, which everyone thought was cute - and I slept on their couch and bummed around and basically had my eyes opened to the whole scene man because Amy worked in a record store on St Mark's Place and that meant we got all of our music for free and because Amy knew people we found we could get into any club for nothing and in most places our drinks were free and if drinks are free you can usually score for free too so between them Kitty and Amy opened my eyes to shall we say a whole world of possibilities. I was what twenty four and I'm in the big city for the first time and my sister and her groovy girlfriend who I suddenly find I'm sort of in love with, truth be told, are taking time out to blow my mind, turning me on to EVERYTHING, dragging me down to the Bleecker cinema to trip through shit like *Chappaqua* and *The Saragossa Manuscript* and I'm reeling, my head is all over the place and just about the only time I get a moment to myself is when I take Glo to Tompkins Square Park where she plays on the swings and I sit on the bandstand watching the world go by, breathing in and breathing out, breathing in New York and breathing out all of the Jodie shit, each and every breath chipping away at the pain and me thinking eventually I'll be okay again, Glo swinging back and forth all the while, back and forth, like some kind of mesmerizing blonde metronome - and me, sitting there, sort of transcendent or at least receptive to whatever it was that the universe wanted to lay at my feet. That's pretty much how I was and how things were when they tripped by, all of the Swami's devotees, the Swami himself at the head of

268

the line, a small Indian man in a bright orange dhoti with a white V painted on his face and all of his young followers, all of the men and the women, all of them chanting *Hare Krishna Hare Krishna Krishna Krishna Hare Hare Hare Rama Hare Rama Rame Rame Hare Hare Hare Krishna Hare Krishna Krishna Krishna Hare Krishna Hare Krishna Krishna Krishna Hare Hare Hare RÃ-ma Hare RÃ-ma RÃ-ma RÃ-ma Hare Hare*, just making this beautiful noise. Jan was the end of the line, twisting and dancing, her hair caught up with flowers, her wide brown eyes full of joy and love and life and she saw me and it was like something clicked or snapped or caught fire or something man because before I knew it she had my hands in her hands and she was tugging me to my feet and I was off and following them, even though Glo was still swinging on the swings, I was off and Jan had me, hook, line and sinker.

The Gift

by Elizabeth Murray

She handed him an envelope decorated with a skull and cross bones; inside sat a hand drawn map with an X that marked the spot. *Skulduggery Swamp* and *Dead Man's Pass* it read in cursive letters of glittered ink, amongst other childish dreams and a poorly thought out riddle. It took seconds to find the treasure wrapped in gold under the bed; a tiny chest filled with chocolate coins and a card which he read, smiling. *"In here you'll find my heart; things easily come and go but love is the only thing worth keeping."* The heart was small, carved out of cheap wood and dyed tomato red; he had to tip out all the coins to find it. He let one of the chocolates melt slowly on his tongue as he nestled the heart back amongst mounds of shiny gold and silver foil, and pulled her close.

The Middlemen

by Tim Horvath

We paired off almost immediately: RJ had anyone that was tall and blonde, Jimmy Duggan got studious brunettes and any with curly hair, and I got whatever was left. We'd talk 'em up a bit, buy 'em drinks, then serve up the stinging truth – we were only the middlemen, reps for guys who didn't go to bars, just auditioning them, yep, it was true. Then we'd whip out the portfolios – fuckin' RJ with his heavy-bond paper and his Publishing Suite Deluxe 3.0. – the newest thing in dating; surprised they hadn't heard of it, not impersonal like online but sweeping aside so much of the b.s., the pick-up lines, the face-to-face sweat-trickle and tongue-tie. Powering through my Guinness, I'd pitch Brian Winters, CEO of a small Medical Supply Company, cyclist, racquetball player, lover of venison with boysenberry glaze, ok, divorced and father of two, did I mention he loves ice-climbing and fishing (yes); do I mention that R.J.'s blended my features into Winters's glossy 5 x 7 so that all the while she's looking at him she's thinking, deep down, about me (nope). At this point, either they're edging away, slightly freaked, thanks but no thanks, or they're wearing big grins like things hastily hung, it goes about 50/50. By now, if they stay I can tell exactly what they're thinking, their thoughts broadcast clear as Jimmy Duggan's goatee bobbing across the room, thoughts like, "I can talk to you, though, the hell with Summers or Autumns or whoever the other guy is, you're funny and cute enough and it's you I'm talking to and so where do we take it from here?"

Corn and Moonlight

by Heather Leet

When I was a teenager I dreamt of getting out of there. The dreams were filled with big cities, exciting jobs and fascinating people. I saw myself in the gleaming city, dancing, working, loving and living the life I knew I was destined for. I did not see myself staying there in that town surrounded by corn, stifled by it, drowned among it, wasted by the corn. So it shocks me each time I pull off the expressway to visit my parents, how it draws me in that corn; the smell of it, the sound of it, the look of it as the moonlight bounces off the glistening ears. It sometimes creeps into my dreams the way the city did before I lived in it, luring me back to that town I swore I would leave forever.

The Den of the Middles

by Doug Wacker

Elvin B. Diddleworth had lived in the Den of the Middles for the last twelve years, before which he roamed the murky pools of the Cambrian swamp, but that was before he was granted the golden gift of consciousness. Yes, the Gods had smiled down upon him on that day, Mizertron with his long beard, wise demeanor, and playful agenda, Yulanda with her youthful figure, long, twisting weave of peppery grey hair, and bronze cane that launched purple firebolts, and, of course, Abberdon, with his red iron helmet, green mustachioed mug, and fancy swerving swagger. Mizertron had been reluctant, for sure, to give the golden gift of consciousness to such a lowly creature as a sac-shaped tunicate, but had been swayed by Yulanda's pleading, well placed in the verses of a festive song. Abberdon had acted as if he disapproved, but, in fact, had persuaded Yulanda to work her magic on Mizertron because Elvin, despite his stationary countenance, was really, quite unknowingly, Abberdon's long lost brother. Abberdon had hoped that Elvin would help him overthrow the fickle and often capricious Mizertron. However, the poor old tunicate instead chose to

274

spend his days ruminating amongst the crusty monks
who slept in the hallways of the Den of the Middles.

Leaving Barstow

by Brian Steel

It's six thirty a.m., and I'm leaving Barstow, heading back into the desert scrub with your midnight laughter in my ears as the sun breaks through the morning and comes galloping over the hood of my car, slapping the windshield like a wave. Ten minutes earlier I was picking my clothes up from the floor of your room. The neon sign of the motel blinked on and off through the cheap, plastic blinds of the window and a lone truck passed on the interstate. And when I turned to leave, you looked back at me with a lazy smile from the twisted sheets of the bed. "Take care," you whispered, and the shadow of a closing door swam gently over your face. We made a balancing act of the night; letting lives and histories and future plans fall away while discovering the smallest details of each other's bodies, crossed in a riot of secret sounds that only find release this sweet, when two lovers first meet, knowing they'll never meet again.

Bunker

by Steve Himmer

Maurice watched every moment for them to bust through his windows or burst from the hearth like too-pious Santas for whom every child is naughty. Since he'd learned from TV - *what was he watching?* - that the Inquisition always comes by surprise, he'd kept himself and his home at the ready. He boarded the windows and stopped up the chimney and put heavy hinges and locks onto his new steel door. He never went out or slept and it was cold in his house without sunlight or fire and all mail rerouted to a PO box unchecked so he wouldn't be followed to his secret address. Friends and relations passed on and were buried, the stock market collapsed and the world was at war, and Maurice huddled with unblinking eyes on a door he hoped was as solid as its website boasted. Even his children stopped calling once they realized there would be no answer because surely the Inquisition is listening and what if it comes through the wires - *turning his own home against him!* - and isn't that just how they'd deliver whatever cruel verdict is his?

He'll Get Better

by Patricia J. Hale

He's a demanding little asshole of a man. In the beginning of our relationship I was scared, then angry and now I'm just tired. I was going to end it all before I really made a commitment, but it was too late and I decided to stick with him. Now he's verbally abusive and he's physically cruel, especially with my breasts. I'm certainly not proud of anything he's done and he can be a whimpering wuss. But I know he'll be a better person than me, my newborn son.

Sad

by Nathan Tyree

There isn't any single word for what I feel at this moment. I am sinking into a Nietzschean abyss of black nothing. I am crushed by a great dead train tearing its way through the night. I'm tumbling in a widening gyre of deaf falcons circling over a rotting corpse planet of shit and decay. I am starting to rust. I am watching my own eyes go dead.

Severed

by Angela Theresa Pitt

The ties that bind are cut, snipped by the shears of the Fates. The unknown waits, poised to engulf the unwitting. Its darkness reaches out, talons clawing and piercing flesh. A battle ensues, wills clashing; a fight for freedom from the black abyss that threatens to control. Light punctures the shroud as it gains a foothold, obliterating it. Severed are the grips of fear and pity as the light brings hope and sustenance.

Thinking of Hannah

by Alun Williams

My daughter's been in the army for just over twelve months. It was her choice and all the family supported her decision. She feels the army can give her something that she wouldn't find here at home. It was the proudest moment of my life when I attended her passing out parade a few months ago. Yesterday she told me she will be going to Afghanistan. I can't stop crying.

How Does My Garden Grow?

by Victor S. Smith

I have a garden. But I don't tend it all the time; sometimes I will let it go for weeks, months or years on end. Sometimes I plant things that don't grow; and sometimes things grow that I don't plant. Ten years ago a beautiful wild flower popped up right in the middle of my garden and I thought it was so pretty that I let it grow there; but then it slowly started to kill off all my other plants and I got angry at it but I couldn't pull it up. Today I trudged out into my garden and grabbed the wildflower by the stem right where it burrows into the ground; and I yanked it, and tugged it and after a mighty effort I got the whole plant, roots and all, out of my garden. Now I am wondering what will grow in place of my beautiful wild flower because after ten years I can't think of anything else there.

Camera Obscura

by Sara Crowley

He is dead, and whilst I haven't seen him in over 10 years anyway, knowing that I never will again leaves, well, less a gap, more a tiny pinhole of dark. There's a jerky old picture reel in my head that shows images of us: brothers in the garden splashing through a hose, his Dinky car, the red one, that I wanted so badly I took it and his fists pounded down on me, and the way he slipped his sausages off the plate and on to mine when we'd get a belt from dad if we didn't eat everything up and the sausages were chewy as a dog leather. There are more but they are all variations on a theme, and really what the fuck am I supposed to do about all this. I can't turn them off and they keep flashing on and on. It's been days now, and still there he is on detention at school, or being booted by the sixth formers for being a weirdo. *Flash, flash* goes the camera, and I tell it to fuck right off, it's got the wrong head, this one has no room for all these pictures, but *click, click,* the film rolls over into the next unwanted image.

Diner Day Blues

by Bryce Carlson

INTERIOR, DINER — MORNING: Sitting alone
at a small, cushioned, 1970s, faded green booth is a
larger man, not morbidly obese but definitely chubby,
drinking a crusty cup of black coffee and picking at
what's left from a messy slice of aged lemon meringue
pie. His fork starts scraping against the ceramic plate,
making a horrific screech that provokes other patrons
to wince, plug their ears, and finish their breakfasts
quicker.   Without   stopping   his   spine-chilling
symphony, the man looks out the window and
watches as a shady looking young man suspiciously
creeps into the parking lot, systematically breaks into
a car, and rides away undetected. An old Asian
woman in the booth behind the man leans over to
complain about the excessive noise but the man is
still transfixed on the window — even without looking
he knows she is Asian because she shouts only in
vowels. As a gothic teen waitress passes by, the man
grabs her attention, causing the old Asian woman to
sit down because she thinks that she is about to be
reprimanded.   But instead, he asks the waitress to
phone the police, causing the old Asian woman to
hurry out of the restaurant, and when the waitress

asks him why, he responds by calmly saying, "I think someone has just stolen my car."

Adrift

by Joseph Grant

When he was five years old, he watched his father
drown. He remembered the feeling of vulnerability
that washed over him as he stood on the sand, the
waves of the bay gently caressing the shore, all the
while his father thrashed in vain to stay afloat on the
surface. As he matured, he blocked certain parts of
his father's confrontation with death out of his mind
with alcohol binges and cheap women; never wanting
to bring to mind that last gasp of breath he witnessed
his father take before going under for the final time.
His relationships with women were continually
tempered with torrents of distrust and arrogance, he
curiously referred to them in nautical terms, a
grueling relationship as having been *a rough crossing* or
as *one angry sea to another* and there was seemingly
always a reference to his feeling *stifled* and *not being
able to breathe.* For reasons unknown to him for a
long time, he possessed an inherent aversion to
oceans and bays, thus, never learned how to swim
properly as he told his psychiatrist years later and
explained that this did not pose a problem, as in his
relationships, he never went in above the waist.
When the tsunami of unblocked memories came

flooding back to him as a result of his therapy, it all became crystal clear; his mother, tired of his father's incessant cheating, had bludgeoned his father's drunken ass with a boat oar and dumped his still-breathing body into the bay and there on the banks he stood and watched helplessly, unbeknownst that he too was already beginning to sink below the first waves of his psychological maelstrom.

Your Future Started Yesterday

by Cate Stevens-Davis

Drink more, he tells her – always, always, urging *drink more*. She tips them back in heavy glass bottles and red plastic cups. Liquid, warm and wet like sex, dribbles out of the corners of her red mouth. It slides over her thin neck, trailing the curves of breasts. Everything with her is soaked, sodden, weighted down. But it doesn't matter, she tells herself; she wasn't going to keep the baby, anyway.

Our American Cousin

by Rod Drake

President Abraham Lincoln knew that his wife was going to have to be institutionalized. He had avoided dealing with this problem as long as he could, even though Mary Todd Lincoln was as crazy as a bed bug, embarrassing him and his administration for years with her lunatic ideas and statements. It was a very sad situation, but acting as the President, not her husband, Lincoln could no longer tolerate it, and with the war ending and a great healing to begin, he had to get her committed to an insane asylum. There was a facility outside of Bryantown, Maryland, only 25 miles away, that she was to be taken to today; the commitment papers were signed, and confidentiality, bordering on wartime secrecy, had been strictly guaranteed. Lincoln, however, decided at the last moment to push the date ahead to tomorrow, letting Mary have one last public appearance as the First Lady, which she so enjoyed. She very much wanted to see the play at Ford's Theater this evening, so he would reluctantly go with her to the performance; with any luck, it would go smoothly, and there would be no repercussions to a final night at the theater.

The Thing About Harry

by Richard Rippon

The thing about Harry is that he's pissed off the wrong people. He left Pauly with eyes like Sly Stallone in *Rocky* and what he did to young Lola was unforgivable. Fay called and said he needed to be put out of the picture, removed from the scene, taken care of. I said I knew some people up North who might be able to take him off their hands, so to speak. She agreed and said it was a shame how things hadn't worked out, how he'd quickly turned friends into enemies... "and that cage with all the tubes cost us a fortune," she said. "Little furry bastard."

Why Tell Me Now?

by Teresa Tumminello Brader

We were together for two weeks, ten years ago, and I'm surprised you remember me. "I could never forget eyes like those," you say, as you stare into them. I think of the time we sat at the bar in Houston's Restaurant, charming the bartender and sampling wines, and you ran your hand up my bare leg under my skirt. I think of the time you unbuttoned my blouse down to my navel and looked up from your fumbling fingers to watch a favorite scene of a rented movie on TV. And I remember that when you kissed me your eyes would drift up and away and I'd try to follow them but I needed a crane. We smile good-bye, and I wonder when you'd ever noticed my eyes.

The Herd

by Adam J. Whitlatch

John scampers on his hands and knees across the
room and presses his back flat against the door,
holding his breath as the thunderous footfalls pass his
door again for the fourth time today. Sweat pours
down his face as the sinister giggling slowly fades
down the hall outside his room along with the
dreaded stomping and bile rises in his throat as he
thinks of the screams that came from the other rooms
whenever they found one of the others, some poor
dumb bastard who snored too loudly or farted at just
the wrong damned time. He listens – eyes darting
back and forth spastically – as the cacophonous
footsteps race from one end of the building to the
other on the floor above him; soon they will be back.
He listened for hours until he eventually dozed off,
but his head suddenly jerks up when he realizes that
it has stopped – the running has stopped and all is
silent, his ragged breathing the only sound. Slowly he
stands and peers out the window of his cell door and
his blood turns to ice in his veins as his eyes fall on
the herd of children standing out in the hall, cruel
and hungry sneers distorting their otherwise beautiful
young faces. At the front of the herd stands a little

boy of about seven years that John instantly recognizes as his own son, and warm urine streams uncontrollably down his leg as the boy – the gap of two missing front teeth showing through his sadistic grin – jingles a large ring of keys and says, "Daddy, come and play with me."

Snow

by Melody Gray

It was past midnight, the illuminating snow stole the darkness from the dead end street. She watched as it covered the ground, like a blanket gently thrown on her bed. She could hear the silence surrounding her, white, muffled and still. Closing her eyes, she tilted her head up towards the sky. Flakes of snow fell softly, melting as they touched her warm skin, tickling her lashes. With a gasp she inhaled, her lungs taking in an icy breath mixed with snow, she heard her son shout "FACE WASH" from behind, her face now covered with the white flakes she had admired only seconds before - *the fight was on!*

Falling Apart

by Bob Jacobs

When I got home from work there was no sign of Gloria, so I fixed myself a microwave Mexican dinner and sat in front of the TV to watch the wrestling. I was tucking into my snack when a thumbnail dropped off, then a fingernail, and I realized to my horror that the rest of my nails were also working loose and my finger joints were starting to weep. I turned up the volume on the TV and hurried into the kitchen to the cupboard where Gloria keeps the first aid kit, by which time my knuckles were bleeding severely and pieces of finger had begun to fall off, leaving behind short, bloody stumps. My fingers were too far gone to open the first aid kit, so I stumbled into the lounge, and as I did so one of my arms fell off at the elbow and the other hung loose from my shoulder. My legs, before they too were reduced to weeping stumps, propelled me towards the table by the sofa where the phone is, and I knew that my only hope was to somehow dial for help, but as I leaned towards the table I saw the note by the phone in Gloria's handwriting. It said, *Bob, I'm leaving you, goodbye*, and I crashed to the floor and completely fell apart without her.

Weight of Wings

by Deborah O'Neal

I have recently acquired both a pair of houses and a pair of doves. The doves, presumably a husband and wife team, follow me from house to house routinely; whichever door I walk out of, I see them. They have lately built two nests - one in the back yard of house number one; the other in a tree overhanging the front walk of house number two - so that now they can live with me, like me. When I take a walk or go for a run, they go too, perching overhead on wires and branches all along my route. I know this pair watches over me somehow, and for some reason; their actions are distinctly purposeful and constant. I only wish they looked happy about it.

In Wrong and Right

by Robert Prinsloo

Some say there is such a thing as life without consequence, and some such a man who says just these sorts of things met me for coffee yesterday at that little place across from that shop that sells things made of used stuff and he told me that there is indeed such a thing as life without consequences, a life in which you can do no wrong because nothing is wrong and nothing is right, it just is, and it's so easy. I said to him "It sounds just swell." He replied "Yeah, but it's not all I crack it up to be, I can tell you." "Unless," he said, drinking all of his black coffee down in one gulp, "unless you surround yourself with people that don't know that there is such a thing as life without consequence, that don't know how to... people who live in right, numbly afraid of being wrong." He gave me a wink, which I took, and a smile, which I did not, for he did have breath on him something foul. So he kept his smile to himself and he said, "And that's why it's been a pleasure, as always, Bob," and having said such he got up and left me there with the bill to pay.

Closure

by Brent Fisk

Late March we let the string slip out and watched
the kite rise and dive again. In my mother's kitchen
garden, autumn's unharvested pumpkins collapsed in
on themselves. My face tightened in the cold as your
hair caught at the corner of your lips. The day
disappeared with the fast moving clouds, a moment
that seemed to mean something: rumble of the
distant trains leaving the plant, lights from the
smokestack blinking off and on, your smile tinged
with the distance of a dream. You turned the wrong
way out of the drive, splash of water near the road.
Your last name began with an M same as other words:
merger, maybe, moving, Monday.

Where is He?

by Linda Courtland

I stand in front of the mirror, reciting affirmations to bring my soul mate closer. I rearrange the furniture per feng shui rules, enhancing my marriage area with a pair of pink throw pillows. I describe him in my journal, using the present tense to show the Universe that I believe my relationship has already manifested. I spend endless hours online, taking personality tests to scientifically match me with the perfect mate. But I still haven't found him and I don't know what to do. Maybe tomorrow, I'll leave my apartment.

No Response

by Mercury

When the accident happened, all those years ago, I used to go and sit beside his bed and talk to him, and when he didn't answer I would come home and cry my heart out. "It's alright," my mother would always say, "it's okay, his brain was damaged, don't expect him to respond," but her words didn't matter to me. He had told me he loved me, told me he would be the one who would catch me when every lover, friend, relative let me down, and he wouldn't just leave me. Not like that. Now, I have stopped expecting a two-way conversation and instead I go and sit by him every day and tell him what is going on with me, so that when he is by himself he can look back on what I have done and have some life to ponder. Everyone says I am expecting way too much of a vegetable, but I know my brother isn't like the rest of the patients in that mental health ward.

The Waiting Room

by Kerrin Piche Serna

There are greasy spots, about twelve inches above the back of each chair, staining the feathery green paint on the wall of the waiting room. These grease spots are head-sized and repetitive with nervous borders. No one has thought to wash them off, or no one has bothered. They wait for the next waiter, the next waxy hairdo, the next sweaty scalp, like holding places on a firing line. They beg your relaxation; they welcome the weight of a heavy head – sit back, close your eyes, others have done so – while you wait your turn. They'll let you go when your name is called but they'll keep a little of you with them, a layer of you to add to their collection, a grimy scrapbook of *Someone Has Been Here*, once.

Part 6

Landing

Fastpass

by Steve Himmer

It was her blue fingertip across his raised palm as she accepted his offering: with that one touch Harold knew. They'd honeymoon in Hawaii the way everyone did, then sell his downtown condo and settle in her suburban home, buy a dog, he'd get her pregnant, they'd wear matching sweaters at Christmas. Children would come one after another until stockings overlapped on the mantle, and those children would fail and succeed at hockey and math, at addicting themselves to one thing or another, and their youngest - Delphine - would overcome a rare form of childhood cancer then pursue a career in medicine. There would be a tradition on each anniversary: a drive on the highway that brought them together, and they'd travel one exit farther each year before stopping to find a hotel, just to see what there was in the world, until one year neither of them felt like driving and they stayed home. She'd keep her job in the tollbooth, she'd insist, and Harold would lose years of sleep to visions of unwashed, anonymous fingers belonging to long-distance drivers leaving their own greasy prints on his wife's open palm. And before the car behind him even had time to honk, Harold knew it was over and sped under the long yellow arm that hung over his head like a sword, merging back into traffic with all the other drivers out driving alone.

Waking Up

by Mel George

She was dreaming he was dead. She was running, but couldn't get to him; she was shouting, but he couldn't hear her; she was crying, and being restrained by unthinking friends. She awoke, her head and heart pounding, and opened her eyes to see the wonderfully familiar walls, feel the comforting warmth of her own bed, the mundane shape of a pair of shoes, and the daylight pressing through the old curtains. For a few seconds a wave of relief washed over her – the sweet relief of the waker who finds herself back in reality and discovers that all her terrors were just a dream. She reached for her phone with a trembling hand, trying to keep that precious moment of reality captive, but failing, as all the unreal messages of the past forty-eight hours stared up at her, unbelievable and fantastic. She thumped her pillow in an agony that waking up had no more power over a nightmare that sat there in the stark light of day, and made normality only a sweet, half-remembered dream.

Angela of Shamrock, Texas

by Brian Steel

As I pass the roadside sign that welcomes me to New Mexico, I'm drawn back to last night, to your Texas eyes and their slices of emerald that shone like wet stones in the dark corners of the hotel bar. I saw the way they burned above the tanned cheekbones of your face, screaming for something better than the driftwood hotels and auto graveyards and the husband shooting pool who you married too young. Last night, your eyes gleamed at me, and your dreams were California stars dancing in the ice cubes of your rum and coke. You should be sitting next to me now as I pass into the desert brush of New Mexico, my navigator through the sun, dreams dusting your eyelids in the daylight, heading for the California coast like a bullet of beauty. But you're back in Texas, in Shamrock, at the hotel desk, still staring at a highway that offers up horizons you're too afraid to touch. You've wrapped yourself in the chains I just threw off; because of your commitment to the family business that lingers on the side of a broken highway; because of your loyalty to a husband whose hands never look for your heart in the dark; because of your overwhelming fear that if you leave, you'll no longer be the prettiest girl in town.

Dear Daughter, Love Dad

by Juliana Perry

The silence was icy in the kitchen as we sat on opposite ends of the island, literally and figuratively; me staring at the grout around the tiles and his rheumy eyes staring through me. Sliding his physician's index finger around the rim of his cut crystal glass he said in a new and rather disturbing tone, "You will atone for your sins." I knew I was in trouble at that moment and my hands shook under the countertop as he spoke words that were foreign to me in our atheist household. I heard the deadbolt slide closed on the master bedroom door; she wouldn't take part in this particular game. He led me to the garage, bent me over the car and had me count while he beat me with a piece of kindling. My father finished, and picking me up, wrapped his arms around my 17-year-old shoulders saying to me "There, there, all better now."

No Matter What

by Nicole Ross

He will remember the little cat noise I make when I yawn, I will remember the strength of his hands. I will think of him when I wear my hair in certain ways, he will think of me as his first, a lot of firsts. I will know that I tried not to be just the first but the best, he will know how he tried to erase the others, the ones who came before him. He will have learned that sometimes, I am emotional for no reason, but that through it I am capable of great passion. I will have learned that once you wake up next to someone you love, sleeping alone is not just alone but lonely. I will need to tell myself that this was real, he will wonder if I still dream about him, if I'm still a little bit crazy.

Stupid Head

by Sara Crowley

In the playground today your son kicked his shoe off his foot and we watched it soar into the air before it landed, *clunk*, on the back of an unsuspecting girl. The girl cried and your stupid headed son smirked. I waited to see what you would do, but you turned away and it was left to me to offer comfort. I gave her a tissue and wiped her tears. "At least you don't have a stupid shaped head like he does," I said. I stared hard at him as he walked into school.

Untitled #3

by Michael Lipkowitz

Eventually the walls of your room were black from the failed photographs you taped up to them, black with the beauty of the entire world. You said you could distinguish one picture from another, but of course I didn't believe you; they were monochromatic, indistinguishable from one another. Still, I remember you pointing to each one and insisting you knew what it was: a black photo of the sunset, a black photo of the dead tree in your backyard, a black photo of the neighbors drinking champagne. I looked at the surrounding black and saw so much, felt so much, except I didn't want to. I wanted to feel nothing. But instead, I felt everything at once.

Flight Home

by Diane Brady

The phone call from Seattle startles me for I hoped you would hang on longer. They said you were at peace, aviation friends by your side, and although you wanted me there, we had already said our goodbyes. Now I am an hour flight from Denver, having breakfast at an airport restaurant. The waitress, noticing my pale face and tears, asks if I'll be OK. I preflight my little airplane and then climb in, but my hands and body shake as I put the key into the ignition, the engine starting easily, prop spinning, ready to go. Today you fly home with me, John, for your presence in the cockpit is evident - I feel you watching over me, keeping the air smooth, the visibility clear, the engine strong; and as I reach my destination safely, I am smiling for I know you have reached yours, too.

Submerged

by Tara Lazar

No one claimed to know her, the woman with the red bathing cap, yet we all watched her, mesmerized by the delicate ripples of her wake, her strokes as smooth and quiet as a scull on a lake at dawn. She entered the pool at exactly 6:35 a.m. each day and claimed the far right lap lane, and we knew to relinquish it to her even if we did not know her name. She was like an ice cube the way she became one with the water, the way she snubbed the other swimmers. One morning the lane remained empty and I found her sitting in the locker room, awash in tears. "Why do we do this — why do we swim?" she asked, and I was unable to respond, oddly flattered that she chose to speak to me. "Please tell me — because all I want to do is drown, and I can't, no matter how hard I try."

(submitted Father's Day 2007)

by Margery Daw

Imagine a guy at work, maybe you think of him as an old lech, maybe he looks the girls up and down. Maybe he finds excuses to hug them. Maybe drunk at an office Christmas party he tried to kiss one. Maybe he makes remarks. Now imagine you're one of those girls, except, instead of at work, he lives in your house. Imagine you're fourteen.

Stolen

by Elizabeth Murray

He lost his eyes to her fingernails that night, but her silence became his angel; his blindness his blessing. He stalks the daytime cloaked in the permanence of viridian green shadows; his sickness hidden behind dark lenses and the tip tap of a thin white stick. His stride fuses into theirs and the cloth of his jacket wafts against their skirts; his sour breath douses necks and stray wisps of hair like dust. Then he takes what they deny him still with the swiftness of a thief, leaving only his stench to remember him by. For no one will blame the blind man. No one.

Noisy Neighbors

by Robert Clay

It seems quite a nice planet, sitting there in the warm zone of a comfortable, stable, if not particularly exciting star. It is the third one out from the star, and has a large solitary moon, which I'm sure must look truly beautiful from the surface. But the dominant species are ill behaved, and above all, they are very NOISY! They live the religion of the bomb, which they construct in vast numbers from small annoying bangs to the brutal reality of the atom. Even worse they transmit radio signals to all points of the sky, on all frequencies, modulated with the most appalling rubbish, which to a species like us, who communicate personally by radio wave, has become unbearable. We are an advanced race, capable of interstellar travel, so we are going to cater to their fetish and show them a bomb much, much more serious than anything they have ever seen, not that they'll see it for long, and then maybe we'll get a bit of peace and quiet in this corner of the galaxy.

To My Soon-To-Be Ex-Husband

by Loobell

Thank you for your explanation, I see you through different eyes; not the eyes of a lover, even a friend, I no longer feel comfort when I see you. When you said that I'd let myself go, not only did you cut me to the quick, but you told a blatant untruth to make yourself feel better about your infidelity. We should be growing old together and enjoying the satisfaction of a job well done, watching our precious children go off into the big wide world. I finally understand what you are, what you have always been and anguish has formed deep in my soul for my lost good years. Well now it's my time, so let me ask you for a favor, you surely owe me one for my years of selfless dedication to you. Hold my towel - I'm taking a well earned dip in Lake Me.

The Vacuum

by Juliann Wetz

Oh, Honey – did turning on the vacuum interrupt your sleep? You were snoring away, so I thought this was a good time to get a little cleaning done, since I found myself awake. I tried to ask you whether it would bother you, but you didn't wake up when I shook your arm, nor when I pulled the pillow out from under your head, and not even when I jumped up and down on the bed ever so gently. I even tried pinching your nose, but you just slumbered away, sawing logs with the same intensity as a chainsaw. You were sleeping so deeply that you didn't even stir when I forgot to turn off the burglar alarm as I let the dog out (and back in). But apparently you can't sleep through the noise of the vacuum; well, now I know.

Theory

by Christen Buckler

.

That strange feeling comes without warning, triggered by the smallest thing. You see a photo of your mother before she gave birth to you, so happy that she's radiating joy off of that yellowed Kodak paper (or, worse still, a photo of both your parents standing together, and all you can see of yourself are a few disjointed features that reside on their own faces: nose, earlobes, cheeks, never your whole face, never your full self) - you are aware that they really existed before you existed, and it astounds you. One day you walk outside and notice how the tiny hairs along your forearm glow in the bright sunshine, like glass is growing through your skin, like you could cut anyone you touch. You look at Saturn through a telescope - or Jupiter, or Mars, or Uranus (the planet that served as catalyst for many sixth grade science class jokes) - and realize how very small you are (microscopic, miniscule, teeny teeny tiny). You wake up one morning, put on your slippers, drink a cup of coffee, go to walk your dog - you see that your front door (your protection, your impenetrable fortress) has been unlocked all night, providing no safety from the ax murderers and child snatchers. You feel it: that punch in the gut, the blood flushing your skin, the nagging *pump pump pump* of your frightened heart; you feel an overwhelming sense that your life matters to no one but yourself in the infinite stretch of time and distance.

Accidents and Slips

by Patricia J. Hale

Being gay, I've had my share incidents where the bigoted and angry take out their frustrations on me. I was naive in not expecting it from my own community. Elizabeth had everything I envied, why did she need to torture me for her enjoyment by exposing those old photos? I never understood why and I'm sure I never will, but I knew that no one else should or would suffer the same fate. It was surprisingly easy, actually, murdering someone in their own home. There are always a host of accidents waiting to happen and her mistake involved smoking in bed and sleeping pills - I, I mean *she*, never should have done that.

Autoerotic Asphyxiation

by Cate Stevens-Davis

I've given it a lot of thought and the best I can figure
it, Mom died as Tyler was helping me tighten the
strap around my throat. We were choking at the
same time; me, holding my breath and smiling up at
him, arching my hips; her, crying maybe, turning
blue, clawing at the tablecloth, desperate. They called
when we were done, when we were both done, and I
was sticky and tangled up in Tyler, stroking his soft
blonde hair. They took care of the details, leaving me
to spend all my time with Tyler, riding the edge of the
blackness. Later, at the funeral, as I looked down at
my frozen mother I was struck with a nagging sense of
jealousy. There lay my mother, so still, holding her
breath for all of forever, and me, on the other side,
filling my lungs.

Another Kodacolor Moment

by Linda Simoni-Wastila

Blurred, my eyes land on the photo: Nantucket harbor, the sunset glowing behind us, a gaudy Mai Tai, while I stare into the camera, serious as the wind whips my hair, but he looks at me, eyes soft, mouth curved in a small smile. I pull the picture from its Lucite frame, gaze at it nestled in my opened hands, and tear it; the rip cleaves his face in two, the smiling mouth interrupted by a jag of white, but then I shred the pieces in half again, and again, until my hand fills with small, ragged-edged papers. The tiny fragments lay in my palm and, for a reason unfathomable to me, I blow, and the soft shards float in the air like dandelion seeds parachuting on a gentle spring breeze, scattering and drifting downward, covering the bed, my slippers, the cracks between floor boards, scores of pieces reflecting his hair and lips and shirt and hands and those malachite eyes. I fall on my knees, scramble to pick them up, but the small bits hover in the invisible drafts created by my outstretched hands, eluding me. God, he'll always be with me. I sob again.

My Cup of Tea?

by Jamie Boyt

I'm a simple chap at heart, easy to please. Books, DVDs, CDs, Pearl Jam and Foo Fighters t-shirts, all good stuff. All things you've given me, things you have spent your hard-earned money on, when you could so easily have gone out and treated yourself. Your generosity astounds me, every day. You seem to know exactly what I want, and just give it to me, for no reason. I just wish I knew who you were; having a stalker can be so damned frustrating.

Always and Forever

by Melody Gray

Your words stung like the whip of a stingray's tail, leaving scars like invisible tattoos etched on my skin. Our mother-daughter relationship was filled with turmoil throughout the last year of your life, and we hadn't spoken in most of that time. Something told me to call you with forgives, and that was when I learned how sick you were; your chances against the cancer were not good. You wanted me to come and place my name on all the special things that I might want once you left us, but I couldn't, because I didn't want believe that it was true. You went back into the hospital, and I got the call from Dad, "You need to come right away, the doctors said Mom only has five days left to live." That was all the time I had left with you, Mom, five days and every last minute to let you know how much I loved you for always and forever.

Marriage Counseling: Perspective 3

by Jennifer Haddock

The woman opens her mouth to speak, but shuts it again when she catches a look from the hostile stranger sitting next to her. She swallows hard against ten years of bile: disappointments, chilling silences, bitter words said in anger that left invisible wounds. The woman makes another mental mark against him when he starts talking about their lack of a sex life. *That really is the only thing important to him, isn't it?* She watches the therapist glance at the clock before saying, "I'm sorry, but your time is up." The woman knows this, in more ways than one.

End

I don't think my life has made any difference. In today's world, most things don't. Superficiality and anonymity are the new world order, embraced by billions of small-minded individuals. My death is strangely ironic. As I lay on the tarmac, crushed, shattered into oblivion, I saw the structure I jumped off for the first and last time in all its purposeful menace. A tall building with a huge billboard saying: DISAPPEAR HERE.

329

Yesterday I Lost My Footing

by Heidi Marshall

Yesterday I lost my footing on ice that looked like the bubbled sheet candy I made in the 7th grade. It was a sidelong, graceful ballet move. At least that's what I'd like to think. Ribs hit first and then my head smacked icy ground. The impact brought a sudden awareness to the design and density of my skull and how it insulates a river of memories. The smooth clear ones that like to flow over slate-colored pebbles and the muddy ones that slide beneath the tease of dark branches.

Dateline: Baghdad

I don't even know why we're here, I said to myself, shivering from the cold as I emerged from another false alarm that I thought had my name written all over it. It wasn't A-Day, the main day of attack, but we could tell the insurrection was ramping up for it, letting us know they had a surge in mind all of their own. Mortar shells exploded across the street, far enough away, but closely sufficient to cover me and my platoon with debris and flying gravel, along with the slight snow that was falling upon us. Only later in the day while our boots on the ground convoy were out on patrol did we discover the main power grid for the city had been hit by the insurgents during the battle, knocking out much of the electric and water for downtown Baghdad. We were quickly dispatched back to the Green Zone as there had been many civilian and military casualties being brought there, and help was needed with the wounded, dying, and the already dead. The civilians we brought to the City Morgue - which had been affected by the power outage; with a shiver I thought for once in the entirety of this fucking war it was good it had been cold.

I'm Going to Die Today

by Adam J. Whitlatch

I'm going to die today, or at least that's what my obituary on page six said; it must be some kind of misprint. It says that I died in a horrible car accident involving a dairy truck, and that I am survived by my parents, my wife, children, and several nephews. But wait, here on page three my horoscope reads, "An event of great importance to you will occur today. Today is a great day to take a nice leisurely drive in the country." You know, it's days like this that make me wish I'd never been born. Good thing I'm going to die today.

Extermination

by E.Y. Kwee

Exterminate. I hate ants, crawling along the white painted window sill, across the granite counter, up the hard corner of the wall, past the slick black ant deathtrap to under my skin; I feel ghosts of a creepy-crawlers on my ear and hand and arm and face and I hate ants. I wash dishes and splotches of burning hot water fall in blotches on the counter next to wriggling black bodies, always wriggling and crawling and moving. Dad speculates that we may have an ant infestation under our house – the line of ants across the smooth kitchen floor has been a thick moving mass for some time now. The ants are sucked up into a black hole of a tube, ringed with rigid black bristles that mop up the ants and spits out a disgusting odor when I lean over the vacuum cleaner, the burning juicy odor of an ant death field. I hope someone remembered to put Raid in the vacuum bag or there'll be some sort of sick surprise later.

The Beast

by Robert Prinsloo

The beast scratched his back against the doorframe and snarled at the woman lying on her bed with her legs apart and her eyes closed. *The bitch wanted it*, the beast thought as he crept closer to the bed and stood over her, sniffing at the air for her scent - vanilla and cigarettes. *Oh, she would get it*, he thought, he'd give it to her! And he'd kill her with it, ripping at her, tearing at her - her neck and her tits and her vagina - and he'd drill her so hard she'd die, and she, clawing at his back with her red, red nails, would beg him to, scream for him to - to murder her harder and harder and harder... but then she opened her eyes and smiled up at him. "Hello, honey," she said, as the beast nuzzled against her belly, his head against her breast. "How was school?"

Fish and Rotary

by Tim Horvath

Somewhere around where 217 merges with 5W I bellow, I mean bellow, *Fuck, the fish*. Twenty minutes later I'm back home pinching the pellet, then watching it descend into the bowl's couple inches of water, downward path like one of those Mercury missions hurtling through earth's atmosphere, caught on grainy film. I have somehow managed not to kill this fish, though I often ask myself if this is not worse, keeping the thing alive but barely, resuscitating it time and time again instead of letting it simply starve off its bones and send purple fish-shrapnel fanning outward and dissolving into the murk. Though I've come back this time - for this alone - I suspect that now I might be strong enough to leave. Each time I go I put more miles between us, and I've circled every rotary and clover-leaf a few times now, teetering at each junction that might boomerang me back or launch me for good. This time I'm back for the fish, and the engine's silent, but I can visualize a spot between two suitcases in the back where the bowl, wedged just so, might hold steady even on the highway.

Coexistence

by Heather Leet

He was being followed, he was sure of it - he thought he had been very careful but apparently not careful enough. He needed to stop and make a plan but he felt so exposed here on the sidewalk, felt as if everyone was staring at him. His tie was askew and his eyes glowed red but really there was no reason for these people to glance at him in horror and then start running. Enough was enough he thought as he turned to the nearest person and blasted him with his laser death ray eyes. "Stop staring!" he yelled as he blasted several more people... "I am not an animal!" The next morning the headlines of every newspaper in the country read: Robot Goes On Rampage As Many Question If Robots And Humans Can Coexist!"

Finding Jesus

by Nathan Tyree

When I was six, my mother found Jesus. I was never really sure how it had happened, but always guessed it must have been when she was vacuuming. I could see her pushing the old Electrolux over the thick shag carpet when the Messiah popped up from behind the couch. That seemed as good a place as any for him to hide. I could picture him peering over the edge of the tan sofa, looking up at my mother with his wide, beatific eyes. Her sacred heart would have melted.

Entr'acte

by Teresa Tumminello Brader

I tell you that I recently married, gesturing to my
husband who stands some distance away, his back to
us, on the phone.   He and I have come to see a
matinee of *The Tempest* even though he's on-call. You
say you're in rehearsals in the Lower Depths Theatre
for a play you've written.   When we were a couple,
you read to me an excerpt of a play you'd started
working on before we met.   Though you didn't read
any of her scenes to me, you said one of your
characters shared my name and perhaps you'd been
prescient. I wonder what became of that girl.

Deep

by Mercury

I have been searching and searching for something deep to write about, something that will set the other writers here off on an insane frenzy of comments praising my abilities. I have been taking every aspect of my life, and other people's, and I've tried to throw them together in a way that is my own, and deep at the same time. I laugh at jokes five minutes after the punchline and run into things a lot. My life is about as deep as a wading pool. People call me ditzy, but I know the deep is in there somewhere. I can feel it.

Etymological Terrorist

by Rachel Green

People see the word *tenterhooks* and imagine a state of excitement; waiting for the postman to call or the telephone to ring. They don't realize that tenterhooks are quite literally barbs used to hold cloth onto a frame for stretching and drying. That's where we at the Dark Fellowship for the Protection of English come in. We teach people the true meaning of the words they bandy about without regard to etymology. Take this gentleman for example, Mr. Peterson; he's becoming very acquainted with the true meaning of tenterhooks, *aren't you?* Excuse me; I'll just wipe the blood from his chin so he can answer...

Sunday Afternoon

by Dawn Corrigan

Once the clothes are turning in the dryers we wander
out of the Laundromat and down to the K Mart. On
our way back an alarm goes off. Someone is breaking
into the Goodyear store. We watch as he darts into
his Dodge pickup truck - gray and maroon, with a
damaged bumper - and speeds out of the parking lot.
A few moments later you say, "Here he comes again.
I hope he's not going to run us over."

Freedom

by Linda Courtland

It enters her body with cyclonic force. First, it lodges in her tear ducts, sealing them shut, making her look tough. Then, it strikes her throat, making it hard for her to speak. It moves to her stomach, causing a pain that can't be diagnosed, and later, it lands on a nest of fragile strings that stretch to hold her heart together. Over the years, it loses some of its fury but gains a more subtle type of strength. And today, the now-transformed secret leaves her lips in a warrior's whisper: "It wasn't my fault."

Precipitation

by Brent Fisk

Gray as the inside of an old oyster shell, his skin
seems steeped in ash. He never flies in his dreams,
his one lung holding him down. On the porch in
winter he steals a smoke and something near sleep as
a soft rain fills the air, blurs the distant streetlights,
the yellow bulb above the pole barn's door. He drops
the cigarette into a soda can, tired hiss of expiration.
Out in the dark cornfields we listen to geese search
for remnant corn. Thinking of spring is a kind of
flight, our hopes for him, a tattered quilt he pulls
close when he can't find warmth.

No Escape

by Rod Drake

It was the same thing, over and over again; I would get home late, which would start an argument between Madeline and I about where I had been. The argument escalates, and after accusations, then much shouting and crying, Maddy storms out of our apartment, only to return an hour later, sheepish and apologetic for the whole silly thing. We would make up, but given her mental instability, everything would suddenly change as I held her, and Maddy pulls a gun from her purse, screaming about the imagined perfume scent that she smells on me. As I struggle to get the gun away from Maddy, it goes off by accident, fatally wounding her. I hold Maddy close as she dies, now sane and herself again, telling me how much she loves me and how sorry she is for everything - I hear sirens off in the distance. The sirens always mark when the time loop starts again, and there I am arriving home late once more.

Reflections on the Wall

by Bryce Carlson

Eyes start to open, it's kind of bright, I have no recollection of what has happened in the last week, oh, and I'm naked and as my eyes adjust, I see a mirrored wall in front of me but wait, every wall is a mirror; in fact, the ceiling and floor are giant mirrors also — all connected by strips of light in the seams so that I can stare at my big old fat self from all angles. I hardly recognize the man who surrounds me in every direction. It's okay, it's okay: breathe, stay calm, don't talk to yourself whatever you do — that's what those bastards want you to do. Damn. Surely, someone will soon realize that there is a full-grown man missing; I mean, hell, I'm somebody, I'm a doctor who knows about band-aids. But come on, this is the worst torture that I could have ever imagined — staring at my ugly unshaven face covered with acne scars and moles that are probably cancerous, dwelling on the hair starting to grow from my nose and ears, noticing the build up of dirt under my finger nails, focusing on my little baby penis, gagging at the sight of my own curly body hair, watching myself defecate because I can't hold it any longer, looking at exactly the kind of man that I have become.

Down

by Kerrin Piche Serna

They saw her fall, of course they did. She came out of the grocery with bags all asunder and her ankle twisted suddenly and she went down, it happened like the forgetting of a dream – there, then gone. They all three saw it, all three boys who were clean-collared and scrubbed with goodness, these young future doctors, lawyers, MBA holders. She lay on the ground with her purse spilled out and her arm bent under her and her coat flayed open, and the cold pavement had opened up a place on her stockinged knee and found a little blood, and they saw this too. They approached from the parking lot like a pack of angels, a gang of saviors, with their shirttails tucked and blue eyes sparkling. Blue eyes sparkling as they darted around, from the Heap of Woman to the lifeless store to the parking lot silent but watching, to the blood to the purse to each other, then to the automatic doors ahead of them as they walked purposefully on, stepping over her body with a great deal of care.

Don't Stop Believin'

by Peter Wild

Ethel and Hymen had a unique story, the kind of story that - when trotted out, at Hog Roasts and such - was just about guaranteed to still conversation, any conversation, taking place within earshot. For a start the two of them were born on the same day, June 21, 1931, albeit over half a world away from one another (Ethel birthed somewhere roundabout Peach Springs in Arizona so her Chihuahuan mother told her, a disappointing norm in a family of carnies who traveled around the Dustbowl performing for nickels and dimes - or stealing nickels and dimes (or chickens and whatever didn't happen to be tied down) when times grew a little rougher and people found themselves too low to enjoy entertainment no more; Hymen was born several thousand miles away in Westfalen in Germany, part of a large Jewish community in the city of Blankenheim, a year or so prior to Hitler's ascension to power (although it seemed to Hymen that Hitler was there, a brooding presence somewhere to the right of his mother's naked shoulder, the instant he opened his eyes for the first time). Ethel spent much of her childhood dreaming of a kink, something that would set her

347

apart, praying for a way to truly belong to her family, sose she could earn just as sure as her rope-necked sister and two-headed brother did, while Hymen was dutiful, quiet, fearful sometimes when he overheard snatches of the adults' conversation (conversation that revolved increasingly around what was happening elsewhere, broken windows and name-calling and ghettoes and violence), the thundering hum of the jackboot building like voltage in their ears, his father growing old fast, his mother's sunken eyes trying to smile in spite of everything, the quiet desperation and earnest frenzy he saw all about him contributing to a sense Hymen developed that life was short and mostly unpleasant. Fate being what it is (and God, both Ethel and Hymen's Gods, different as they were, being the kind of deities who like to give even as they take away), each suffered in their own private and peculiar way: Ethel, for example, was struck by lightning at the age of nine whilst helping to set up the tent in a farmer's field south of Thermopolis and rendered completely hairless (prone at the most inopportune moments to both smoking and sparking), a gift that rapidly palled in her adolescence as she grew to realize she'd more than likely live her life alone, without the love of a good man behind her; roundabout that time, Hymen was taken along with his family and something in the region of 350 other Blankenheim Jews, men, women and children all, and marched for the better part of two and a half days to a lime pit just shy of the Belgian border where a battery of SS men shot each and every one of them in the head. Remarkably Hymen didn't die although he lay, conscious beneath ten times his own body weight of corpses for what felt like a week but couldn't have been more than a day, his head quietly throbbing from the bullet lodged harmlessly in his brain (a bullet, one of several thousand of similar inferior quality, stolen from a retrograde Russian munitions factory in the Belarus) and the smell of blood and vomit and rotting meat thick in his nostrils. Was fifty years before Ethel and Hymen even met each other (fifty unhappy years spent staring out of porthole windows and moving cars, howling inside for some kind of something, traveling from here to there and from there to some other place and from some other place to still some other place, all places turning out to be much like the place you'd left, all places as cold and haunted as the grave), their eyes catching with the whoomph of petrol taking light at a line dancing conference of all things in Modesto, California - the rest, as they say, looking at each other, smiling and twinkling, arms about each other's waist, the slow waft and drift of Hog Roast in the air, is history.

Analogy

by *Shaindel Beers*

What she needs him to understand is that to a girl from a nowhere town, marriage is the female equivalent of joining the military; if he were in her classroom, she would write in dark blue dry erase marker on the white board, "Early marriage is to women as joining the military is to men." It is as simple as "leaf is to tree as feather is to bird," but she cannot get him to understand that society still does things like this to women. If you are a boy, you can, "visit exotic places, meet fascinating people, and kill them;" if you are a girl, you can, "move from your father's house to another man's house, cook and clean for him, and pray for an early death." She has wanted to explain the intentional crashing and burning of her first marriage as trying for a dishonorable discharge because there was no other end in sight; of course no one thinks an affair is a good idea, just like no PFC thinks holding his .50 caliber machine gun pointed at his chest and screaming *Get me out of this fucking war or I'll do it myself!* is a good idea; but sometimes it's the only way out. To her, domesticity and war have always seemed analogous to one another; for years she has wanted to write something important and scholarly connecting women dying in childbirth and men dying in battle as being the same thing, essentially. But all she gets are blank stares; don't they even teach analogies anymore — even for the SAT — isn't anyone capable of critical thought?

The Seventh Sentence

by Robert McEvily

My crew and I traveled a great distance to meet a woman named Totem. In a convincing ad in *Psych* magazine, Totem claimed to have the answers to all of life's questions. My crew and I had the same question: *What is true happiness?* As if a fog had lifted, her reply made clear and perfect sense. It altered the courses of our lives. This is what she said, word for word:

About the Authors

Silvi Alcivar recently graduated from Penn State's MFA program with a concentration in creative non-fiction writing. She lives in San Francisco.

Scott Beal was *826michigan*'s Volunteer of the Month in November 2007.

Shaindel Beers hasn't become "Tiny Girl Violence" yet. But at 5'1" and 115 pounds, she's thinking about it. *Really* thinking about it. She lives in Oregon.

Jamie Boyt is a 32-year-old IT worker from the Southeast of England, who firmly believes that - despite lack of ideas and motivation (not to mention talent) - a bestselling novel is living inside him somewhere (if he can just find someone to write it for him).

Teresa Tumminello Brader was born in New Orleans and lives in the area still. Her stories have appeared in *The Ranfurly Review*, *Octaves Magazine*, *971 Menu*, and *Debris Magazine*.

Diane Brady is a former Alaska journalist and a pilot of 29 years. She currently lives in Denver, Colorado.

Quin Browne lives in New York City. She likes it there.

Christen Buckler is a junior at Florida State University. If she can't make a million dollars with her writing by the time she graduates, she is going to become a high school English teacher. She hopes to teach the youth of America how to fight *The Man* and how to find themes of light and dark in *The Scarlet Letter*.

Jon Cable tries to escape, but always winds up tangled in rusty swords and cloudy-eyed dragons.

caccy46 is a mother of two who's been married for 32 years.

Maura Campbell is a PR pro and part time writer who just moved to her dream house (and garden) in suburban Detroit, where she sits surrounded by several new pieces of IKEA furniture, trying hard to live a good life (and making great new memories).

Bryce Carlson recently graduated from Chapman University and now lives as an aspiring screenwriter in Southern California.

Raquel Christie is an editorial assistant in New York City and an aspiring novelist.

Robert Clay is a Seafarer now stranded on land. He lives in Cornwall in the UK.

L.R. Cooper is a middle aged frustrated writer trying to get the creative juices back after having raised her kids to adulthood.

Dawn Corrigan's work has appeared recently or is forthcoming at *Bound Off*, *Glitter Pony*, *The Smoking Poet*, *Cautionary Tale* and *Monkeybicycle*, and continues to appear regularly at *The Nervous Breakdown*.

Linda Courtland is a fiction and travel writer based in Los Angeles. She's thrilled to be included in this fabulous, first-ever *Six Sentences* book!

Sara Crowley is (in no particular order) a mum, writer, daughter, bitch, sister, friend, bookseller, and wife.

Dark Icon spawned spontaneously from his own imagination 36 years ago, and has spent the majority of his time trying to write himself out of existence, with varying degrees of success.

Jason Davis is a biologist who lives and works in Seattle. In 2008 he will be in Tibet, studying the art of the hidden pencil (and birds too).

John Parke Davis's work has been published in *Ideomancer*, *flashquake*, and *Shimmer Magazine*. By day, he's an attorney.

Margery Daw is a pseudonym and part of a nursery rhyme.

Rod Drake's stories have appeared in *Flashes of Speculation*, *Fictional Musings*, *Flash Flooding*, *Flash Forward*, *MicroHorror*, and *AcmeShorts*.

Megan Elliott is a writer and editor. She lives in Brooklyn, New York.

Elizabeth Feldman is just an average mommy living in an interesting town.

Brent Fisk is from Bowling Green, Kentucky. His stories have been published in *Prairie Schooner* and *Debris*, and his poems have won the Sam Ragan Prize and the Willow Award. He received an Honorable Mention in *Boulevard*'s Emerging Poets Contest, and is a four-time Pushcart nominee.

Sarah Flick calls 'em as she sees 'em.

Monica Friedman is a professional writer/starving artist. She reads consummately and indiscriminately.

Mel George lives in three cities at the moment (but she still likes Oxford the best).

David Gianatasio's book of fiction and commentary, *Swift Kicks*, was published last year by So New Publishing.

Barry Graham is a simple man, who writes about simple things, very simply. His fiction has appeared most recently in *Storyglossia*, *Pindeldyboz*, *Hobart*, and *Prick of the Spindle*.

Joseph Grant is originally from New York City and currently resides in Los Angeles. He has been published in over 55 literary reviews and e-zines, such as *Byline*, *New Authors Journal*, *Howling Moon Press*, *Hack Writers*, *New Online Review*, *Indite Circle* and *Cerebral Catalyst*.

Melody Gray lives in Canada. She spends most of her time reading, writing, and in her garden.

Rachel Green is an English woman who spends far too much time writing about demons.

Jennifer Haddock is a happily married wife, a mother, a part-time psychotherapist, and a wannabe writer. She lives outside Baltimore, Maryland.

Patricia J. Hale has had stories published in *Powder Burn Flash*, *Flashshot*, *Flash Pan Alley*, *MicroHorror*, *Fictional Musings* and *Apollo's Lyre*. She writes because she can't stop herself. Her husband can't stop her either.

Tommy Hall lays down his life. Do with it what you want.

Lee Herman is a remodel carpenter who records life lessons in a little black book when nobody's looking. He lives in Pendleton, Oregon, with the writer, Shaindel Beers.

Steve Himmer's stories have appeared in *Ghoti*, *Monkeybicycle*, *Juked*, *Pindeldyboz*, *Brevity & Echo* (Rose Metal Press), and *A Field Guide to Surreal Botany* (Two Cranes Press).

Peter Holm-Jensen is an émigré living in the UK.

Tim Horvath is a New Hampshire-based writer with stories published in *Carve*, *Eclectica*, *Sleepingfish*, and elsewhere.

Bob Jacobs lives in the southeast of England with his wife and kids and Sony Vaio. In his spare time, he likes to lie motionless on his back, whistling and staring at clouds.

Saif Khan is an undergrad at Penn State who was inspired by his former ethnography teacher to start writing. He will earn a minor in English at the end of the spring '08 semester.

Andrew David King has been published in many print and online publications, as well as alongside authors Ursula K. Le Guin and Luis J. Rodriguez. He lives in Fremont, California.

Christopher Kirk is an undergraduate majoring in journalism at Northwestern University.

E.Y. Kwee is unfortunately college-bound. Otherwise, she'd spend the rest of her life walking on the beach.

Emma J. Lannie was born in Manchester and moved to Derby after University. She's worked in bars, played in bands, written punk fanzines, managed a bookshop, and now divides her time between her library job, writing, and traveling.

Amanda Lattin is a chemistry teacher and a certified aromatherapist in Portland, Oregon. She is presently working on a master's degree in herbal medicine and aromatherapy, and enjoys writing as a luxurious escape from school and motherhood.

Tara Lazar loves trying to compose witty bios that make her sound interesting, but often fails.

Heather Leet likes to write very short stories in her spare time; she considers it an art form. She does not make a living writing her very short stories (but a girl can dream). She does make a living selling world peace to unsuspecting Americans and hopes one day that her job will be obsolete.

Arris Leighton lives in Southern California and spends her time staying under the radar.

Michael Lipkowitz moonlights as "Ed's Poofed Hair."

Loobell (*harassed middle-aged mother, badly lapsed blogger*) is fed up with taking the blame.

Rolland Love is the author of award-wining short stories, novels, and a bestselling computer resource directory. He is co-author of *Homegrown in the Ozarks: Mountain Meals and Memories*, which led to his appearance on a FOX TV cooking show. He lives in Overland Park, Kansas.

Linda Lowen, who regards the act of writing as akin to baking, toils round-the-clock to produce her daily bread - anything and everything relevant to women's issues for her readers at About.com.

Sophia Macris likes owls, James Merrill, and tequila shots.

Montgomery Maxton lives day to day as best as he can.

Robert McEvily is the creator and editor of *Six Sentences*. He lives in New York City and totally loves Jill.

Peggy McFarland celebrated eight years of smoke free living on January 20th, 2008.

Monica McFawn's poetry and fiction have been published in *Conduit*, *Conjunctions*, and *Poetry Salzburg Review*.

T.J. McIntyre is a writer of speculative and literary fiction from Alabaster, Alabama. His work has appeared recently in *The Swallow's Tail*, *55 Words*, and *Escape Velocity*.

Mercury likes to sound all deep and experienced when she writes. She also likes blowing bubbles, and painting her toenails rainbow colors.

Jennifer Moore's fiction and poetry have appeared in *Mslexia*, *Pulp Net*, *The First Line*, and the Route 16 anthology *Wonderwall*. She lives in Devon, England.

A.R. Morgan has been fumbling through the writing process for most of her life. She hopes to eventually hit her stride.

Elizabeth Murray writes about poker and casino for a living. Her ultimate ambition is to swim with great white sharks and write a published novel. She lives in the South of Spain.

Tharuna Niranjan will keep trying to impress upon her son the lofty ideals of vegetarianism.

The Old Guy Up Front is retired, still writing, mostly poetry. He's an appalled Southern Liberal Democrat.

Deborah O'Neal is writing again after 17 years in the doldrums.

Juliana Perry is a single mom of three, a lover of all things wine, cheese and bread, a maintainer of all things house and home, a student of business and psychology, and a professional scheduler and multi-tasker.

Rebecca Pigeon lives and works in Washington. She believes the works of Willa Cather should be required reading for everyone. (She can be kind of dogmatic that way.)

Sherrie Pilkington, 43, has been married for 21 years. She's the mother of two boys who participate in extreme sports.

Angela Theresa Pitt has an endless curiosity for words. She's constantly amazed by how much can be said with so little.

Don Pizarro's work has appeared online at *American Nerd*, *Byzarium*, and *McSweeney's*.

Robert Prinsloo's stories have been published on *Dogmatika*, and included in the Carbon Copy Commodity Exhibition at Bell Roberts Cube Gallery in Cape Town.

Richard Rippon lives in the northeast of England. His writing has appeared in *Cautionary Tale* and *Mannequin Envy*.

Ian Rochford, a screenwriter, recently rediscovered the pleasures of writing short stories. He lives in Australia.

Nicole Ross is excited to be part of this first-ever 6S book!

Harry B. Sanderford is a Central Florida surfing cowboy who'd sooner spin yarns than mend fences.

Darrick H. Scruggs tries to help people overcome adversity and obstacles.

Kerrin Piche Serna's short fiction has appeared in the *Los Angeles Times* and the *Portland Review*.

Oceana Setaysha is a 16-year-old girl living with her family at the top of Australia. She considers herself a writer, a poet, an artist, and a musician. (People keep telling her to be more realistic.)

Chi Sherman is an Indianapolis-based writer who often fantasizes about owning a three-bedroom house in which the guest room is a pale-yet-deep shade of the lightest blue.

Linda Simoni-Wastila is a number-crunching, ivory tower type by day; at night, she powers up the other side of her brain and catharses words. She is currently writing her second novel, *Pure*, a tale about ethics and perverse incentives found in the hallowed halls of higher learning.

Victor S. Smith, who thinks *Big Trouble in Little China* is the best movie ever, loves using two spaces after a period.

Eric Spitznagel is a regular contributor to magazines like *Playboy* and *The Believer*. He's also the author of six books, the most recent being *Fast Forward: Confessions of a Porn Screenwriter*.

Brian Steel is a poet and writer living in Baltimore, Maryland. He is currently working on a novel and a collection of Flash Fiction pieces.

Cate Stevens-Davis is an MFA candidate and Rachel Carson Fellow at Chatham University in Pittsburgh, Pennsylvania.

Samuel Sukaton represents the Blue and Gold of UCLA.

Steve Talbert, a fan of cereal box copy, loves reading and writing microfiction. His work has appeared in *55 Words*, *55Fiction*, *Pen Pricks* and *MicroHorror*.

Abigail Levin Tatake is a teacher, writer, and merrymaker in Seattle, Washington.

Nathan Tyree's work has appeared in *Flesh and Blood*, *Doorknobs and Body Paint*, *The Flash*, *Bare Bone*, *Dogmatika*, *Wretched and Violent*, and *The Empty Page: Stories Inspired by the Songs of Sonic Youth*.

Philip Alexander Rex Velez is a part-time writer, a freelance photographer, and a full-time businessman.

Doug Wacker, an avid member of *The Drinklings*, is an adjunct professor in the Biology Department at Seattle University. He lives with his lovely wife Kim, daughter Eilidh, and two persnickety cats, Luna and Nimbus. He is currently working on his yet-unnamed debut novel about paternal betrayal, hyperborean self-exile, and the lives of three brothers.

Juliann Wetz is the author of two Robbie & Marshall adventures: *Boot Camp* and *Genuine Swiss Army*. Her work has appeared in *Highlights for Children*, *Daughters Newsletter*, *Boys Life*, *Capper's*, *Good Old Days*, *Personal Journaling*, and *Child Life*. She also writes for the Cox Newspapers of southwestern Ohio.

Maggie Whitehead enjoys writing, reading, chocolate-covered strawberries, sunsets, and navel-gazing. She's a high school English teacher, and lives with her husband and their mildly aggressive dog in suburban Detroit.

Adam J. Whitlatch is the author of numerous short stories, the novel *The Blood Raven: Retribution*, and the novels-in-progress *E.R.A. – Earth Realm Army* and *The Weller: Tales of the Wastelands*. He lives in Iowa.

Peter Wild is the co-author of *Before the Rain*, and the editor of *The Flash* and *Perverted by Language: Fiction inspired by The Fall*.

Alun Williams lives in Wales. He writes in *Critters Bar* and *Zoetrope* under "maxie slim" and "Maxwell Allen." Several shorts by Alun have been published in *Write Side Up*, *Cambrensis*, and *Secret Attic*.

Alana Wilson is a full-time college student, mother, wife, caregiver, and slave to her extended family.

Karl Winklmann lives in Boulder, Colorado. He does not own any sheep nor is he the guardian of any sheep as defined by the Boulder City Council.

Rob Winters is an undergraduate English Literature and Creative Writing student at the University of Westminster.

Li-Ann Wong, before migrating to Sydney, Australia in her mid-teens, was born and bred respectively in Ipoh and Perak, Malaysia. She currently majors in Law and Commerce at Macquarie University in Sydney. She is a self-professed bibliophile, jazz cat, dessert addict, and Old Soul (having reached the ripe ol' age of 21).

Andrew Woodward is a fan of Beowulf.

Stephanie Wright is a social psychologist on faculty at Coastal Carolina University in Conway, South Carolina.

Louise Yeiser studies Creative Nonfiction at the University of Pittsburgh, and prefers comfy coffee houses to art exhibits. She lives in Sewickley, PA.

Miz Yin is a 19-year-old college student who has changed her major four times (and thinks she may become an English teacher). She loves writing more than anything. Even video games.

Madam Z loves six and isn't afraid to admit it.

Author Blogs and Websites

Sara Crowley
asalted.blogspot.com

Dark Icon
darkicon.com

Jason Davis
thestorygame.googlepages.com

John Parke Davis
thestorygame.googlepages.com

Monica Friedman
dragonslibrary.blogspot.com

Mel George
thepygmygiant.blogspot.com

Barry Graham
dogzplot.com

Rachel Green
leatherdyke.co.uk

Patricia J. Hale
patriciahale.blogspot.com

Peter Holm-Jensen
notesfromaroom.wordpress.com

Steve Himmer
tawnygrammar.org

Andrew David King
andrewdavidking.blogspot.com

Emma J. Lannie
garglingwithvimto.blogspot.com

Tara Lazar
anonymom.wordpress.com

Rolland Love
ozarkstories.com

Linda Lowen
womensissues.about.com

Montgomery Maxton
montgomerymaxton.blogspot.com

Robert McEvily
sixsentences.blogspot.com

Monica McFawn
litandart.com

T.J. McIntyre
southernfriedweirdness.blogspot.com

Jennifer Moore
jennifermoore.wordpress.com

A.R. Morgan
gogoonapage.blogspot.com

Elizabeth Murray
serendipitypoetry.com

The Old Guy Up Front
theoldguyupfront.blogspot.com

Linda Simoni-Wastila
leftbrainwrite.blogspot.com

Oceana Setaysha
setaysha.blogspot.com

Victor S. Smith
likepollution.blogspot.com

Eric Spitznagel
vonnegutsasshole.blogspot.com

Cate Stevens-Davis
fathounddog.com

Doug Wacker
drinklings.googlepages.com

Adam J. Whitlatch
myspace.com/xtreme_studios

Peter Wild
peterwild.com

Stephanie Wright
thehallofmirrors.com

Madam Z
z-to-u.blogspot.com

372

What can *you* say in six sentences?

sixsentences.blogspot.com

763807

Made in the USA